BREAK into the INTERNET!

PICK YOUR PLAYER, START YOUR QUEST

By **Carla Jablonski**

Illustrated by the **Disney Storybook Art Team**

DISNEP PRESS

LOS ANGELES • NEW YORK

Printed in the United States of America
First Hardcover Edition, October 2018
1 3 5 7 9 10 8 6 4 2
ISBN 978-1-368-01215-7
FAC-038091-18236
Library of Congress Control Number: 2018945178
For more Disney Press fun, visit www.disneybooks.com

SUSTAINABLE FORESTRY INITIATIVE   Certified Sourcing
www.sfiprogram.org
SFI-00993
Logo Applies to Text Stock Only

THIS IS NO ORDINARY BOOK!

First of all, the story takes place *inside* video games and the Internet. You'll meet characters from the games *Fix-It Felix, Jr.*, *Sugar Rush*, and more.

You'll even *be* one of them!

That's right! What makes this book truly different is that YOU are part of it! Every now and then, you'll be asked to make a choice. And that choice will affect what happens next.

Choose wisely. Your choices will determine if you win the Internet or it's game over!

But first you need to choose **who** you'll be for this exciting adventure.

Are you **Vanellope von Schweetz**, super-duper *Sugar Rush* racing kart driver and noted troublemaker? Then start your engine and your adventure on **PAGE 196**.

Or are you **Wreck-It Ralph**, the lovable lug and Bad Guy par excellence from *Fix-It Felix, Jr.*? Then stomp on over to the **NEXT PAGE**.

Well? What are **you** waiting for?

RALPH

While Ralph is technically the **Bad Guy** in his beloved classic arcade game, he's actually a **big softie** IRL.

VANELLOPE

The **fastest racer** in *Sugar Rush*, Princess Vanellope is quick, sharp, and always **ready for adventure**— especially with her best pal, Ralph.

FIX-IT FELIX, JR.

If something needs fixing, Felix should be your first call. He's got a **magic hammer** and a **big heart**, both of which are made of **gold**.

YESSS

No one's more on the pulse of what's popular than Yesss—she knows **what's in** and **what's out**, and you'll always find her on the leading edge of the latest trends.

GENE

He may not be the **nicest Nicelander**, but Gene cares deeply about *Fix-It Felix, Jr.* and he's always looking out for what's **best** for the game.

YOU ARE RALPH

AKA **WRECK-IT RALPH,** the Bad Guy from the classic arcade game *Fix-It Felix, Jr.* Your job is to smash things. Felix's job is to—that's right!—fix what you broke.

You have to admit, in the past you were pretty unhappy. You didn't mind the work—smashing things is cool. But everyone else in your game enjoyed each other's company and sharing pie. You lived all alone on a pile of bricks in the dump. Not exactly what you'd call a glamorous life. In fact, even though the people in your game are called *Nice*landers, they weren't very nice to you.

Then you met **Vanellope von Schweetz**. She's a driver in *Sugar Rush*, a racing game on the other side of the arcade. Things weren't so peachy at the beginning. At first, Vanellope kind of annoyed you. She kept getting in the way of your goal to earn a medal. But she wore you down and grew on you. Like a fungus.

Turn to **PAGE 9.**

Suddenly, a shadow falls over you both.

"Hey, where'd our sunrise go?" you ask, confused.

Beep, beep, beep!

"Oh my gosh!" Vanellope says. "That's the plug-in alert. Litwak's plugging in a new game!"

Other characters gather nearby, trying to get a look.

"Ooh, we gotta go check it out," Vanellope says.

She glitches up onto your shoulder. You turn toward the socket that will be used for the new plug. Felix from your game and his wife, Calhoun, from *Hero's Duty*, are already there. Others are rushing to the spot. Everyone is eager to find out what new device Mr. Litwak has brought to the arcade. **Plug-in days** are always exciting.

By the time you and Vanellope make it to the socket, a crowd has gathered. "Coming through," you say as you shove your way to the front. "Move it or lose it."

"Please be a racing game. Please be a racing game," Vanellope murmurs atop your shoulder.

A hush falls over the crowd as Litwak's hand brings a plug to the socket.

Find out what it is on PAGE 164.

You pass rows and rows of booths, all selling amazing—and not-so-amazing—stuff. Ralph moves so quickly it's all a blur. You keep your eyes on your destination: the **Vintage Arcade Games** booth.

Then Ralph slows down as he spots an intriguing item. "Hey, don't you think a potato shaped like a tomato would make a wonderful addition—ow!"

He rubs his head where you thwapped it.

"Focus, dude," you scold. "We have a steering wheel to get and a deadline to meet!"

"Fine, fine, fine," he mutters.

Turn to **PAGE 123.**

4

YOU ARE SOMEONE ELSE

IT MAKES SENSE for someone to keep an eye on things in the arcade while Vanellope and Ralph track down that steering wheel. But who should be holding down the fort?

If you think Felix is a good choice, turn to PAGE 66.

If you choose Gene to take care of things while Ralph and Vanellope enter the mysterious internet, turn to PAGE 165.

You watch as Vanellope trundles back to *Sugar Rush*. You feel . . . unsettled. It sounds as if Vanellope is **bored**. Bored with her game. Maybe even bored with *you*.

For the first time, you're out of sync. Example? You *like* routine. You like having things you can count on.

But Vanellope seems to be craving new experiences. Could that mean she also wants to make other friends?

Maybe if her game was more **challenging** she'd feel more content. With everything. Including you.

A plan formulates in your brain. "Brilliant," you tell yourself. "Even if I do say so myself."

That's it! You figured out what to do. You're going to go into her game and make it more challenging. But how?

"Hmmmm." You stroke your chin as you consider your options.

If you decide to enlist characters from the other games to add surprises to Sugar Rush *when the drivers race after the arcade is closed, turn to* PAGE 13.

If you decide to change up the track in time for the arcade to open, turn to PAGE 21.

"Whaddya say?" You clap your hands and grin, trying to get them pumped up. "Try something **new**. Just think, brand-new kids to terrify!"

That catches their attention. A few nod. Zombie smirks. Even Sour Bill's usual frown seems a bit more cheerful.

"Do we have to drive those silly cars?" Cyborg, the powerfully built half robot, asks. "There's no way I can squeeze into one of those tiny things."

"I never learned how to drive," Satine whispers.

Even with that red skin, you can see that he's blushing.

"Not a problem," you assure them. "What I have in mind are some **surprise ambushes**. You know. Jump out and scare. You're all so good at that." You figure giving them compliments will help. Bad Guys rarely rake in the kudos.

"Can we wear dark glasses?" Sorceress asks. She tucks a strand of her long dark blue hair behind one of her pointed ears. "The colors in that game are so bright they could blind a person."

"I'm sure that can be arranged," you say.

After answering more questions, you're pleased to see that you have some volunteers.

"Great!" you say. "Tomorrow night after the arcade closes, you five meet me at the entrance to *Sugar Rush*."

Go to the NEXT PAGE.

The next night, you start to worry as you approach *Sugar Rush*. Your Bad Guy volunteers are already waiting by the plug, as promised. Somehow, they look bigger and scarier than they did at the **Bad-Anon** meeting.

Will they be too frightening for the drivers in *Sugar Rush*? They're just kids, after all. And *Sugar Rush* has never had any Bad Guys. The drivers aren't going to know how to handle it.

But you're determined to make the game more interesting for Vanellope. Having Bad Guys jump out at the drivers as they zoom along the track will definitely make things more—what was the word she used? Oh, yeah. *Challenging*.

Bad Guys *always* make things more challenging. It's how you're all designed. It's in your code!

Turn to PAGE 201.

"I think we have to **trap** Surge," you whisper to Vanellope.

"How do you propose we do that?" she asks.

"We can lure him into that closet," you say, pointing. "Then we shut the door and lock it. Harmless."

Vanellope considers for a moment, then shrugs. "Not bad, Sir Stink. But isn't he going to be mad when we get back?"

"We'll cross that bridge when we get to it."

Vanellope beams at you. "I like your style, pal o' mine!"

Turn to PAGE 58.

Together, you changed things for each other. An error in her code makes Vanellope **glitch** sometimes. That made her something of an outcast in her game. But you helped her discover that she's actually a *princess* in *Sugar Rush* and didn't even know it!

You were afraid a fancy princess with a tiara and petticoats wouldn't want to be friends with an overall-wearing big galoot like you. But to your relief, Vanellope isn't the froufrou and la-di-da sort of princess.

The Nicelanders realized what an amazing, fantastic, and all-together awesome hero type you really and truly are. Now they are living up to their name. They're being *nice* to you!

Back in your own game, you still wreck things and Felix still fixes them. Only now, you're in it together. You are 100 percent accepted. Just like Vanellope is in *Sugar Rush*.

Even better—you and Vanellope are true-blue best friends.

Turn to the NEXT PAGE.

Every night, as soon as Litwak's Family Fun Center closes down, you and Vanellope leave your games. You meet up in **Game Central Station**—that's the power strip where all the different games in the arcade are plugged in. It's a huge, cavernous space. When the arcade is open, it's pretty quiet, since all the characters are in their games, playing their hearts out for the human customers spending their coins. But once the arcade closes for the evening, Game Central Station is packed with game characters taking the tram down the wires and out of their plugs. They visit each other's games, they lounge on the benches, and they catch up on news.

And that's where you and Vanellope engage in all kinds of goof-offery. At the end of every night of good-hearted mayhem and mischief, you sit together and watch the sunrise through the sockets of an old empty plug.

You can't imagine life being any sweeter. You want things to continue just like this, each and every day, forever and ever.

Today you and Vanellope sit on your favorite bench in Game Central Station, celebrating the **sixth anniversary** of the day you met. Time sure flies!

Go to the NEXT PAGE.

You sit side by side, watching the sunrise, talking as you watch the light stream in.

"So you're saying there's not one single solitary thing about your life that you would change?" Vanellope asks.

"Not one," you say. "It's flawless."

She gives you a look.

"Think about it," you say, "you and me get to goof off all night long. Litwak shows up. We go to work. The arcade closes. Then we get to do it all over again. Only thing I might do different would be not having to go to work. Other than that, I wouldn't change a thing."

Watch another new day begin on PAGE 2.

"For this very first trial, I'm not going to drive," you announce. "I'm going to be the judge!"

The drivers gasp. You're even a bit surprised yourself. But you want to see if your idea will work. Squabbling drivers isn't the way to test it.

The teams get worked out. You clamber up into the viewing stand. "Ready?" you shout.

Horns honk in reply.

"And go!" You bring down the flag in a strong, sharp move. ***They're off!***

You watch as the drivers make the first lap; then the next drivers take their turns. Everyone seems to be having a great time. You wish you were out there with them, but if this is going to go the way you think it will, you have a feeling you'll be joining a relay team soon.

Turn to **PAGE 181**.

The more you think about it, the more you like this idea. Maybe other people are bored with their games, too. Throwing a couple of new characters into the mix would add a little **spice** for everyone. They do all get excited when something new is plugged in. New things *can* be fun. So making these changes could be just the ticket. For everybody!

You rub your hands together with excitement. "Yup! A great morale booster!"

You'll be everyone's hero. Maybe even get another medal! Vanellope will be content and not look for challenges someplace else—with someone else.

But who should you enlist for this awesome experiment?

Should you ask the Nicelanders in **Fix-It Felix, Jr.** *to volunteer on* **PAGE 71?**

Or do you attend tonight's Bad-Anon group and ask the Bad Guys there to go into **Sugar Rush** *on* **PAGE 172?**

"Um," you begin, "I have to, uh, reorganize my bricks. It's getting awfully messy at the dump."

"Oooookay." Her forehead furrows as she studies you. "You up to something, Ralph? You're being weird. Even more than usual."

"Nope, just me being me," you tell her. "So, go on. Back to *Sugar Rush*. I know it's all very boring for you. But maybe it will be a bit more *challenging* tonight."

"Maybe you'll be less bizarre tomorrow." She shakes her head, but she goes.

"Maybe," you call after her.

You know at the moment she's kind of upset with you. But once she sees what you've done, she's going to be over the moon.

Go to the NEXT PAGE.

You hurry into the game to watch the hijinks. You climb a candy cane tree for a good view. You spot Calhoun in position just around the first bend. Gene is hurrying to a spot farther along the track. Felix stays low as he sneaks from cotton candy bush to cotton candy bush. You can't wait to see Vanellope's reaction to the surprises.

Sour Bill gives the signal. The drivers take off from the starting line.

"C'mon, Calhoun," you whisper. She's the first surprise the drivers will face in this Ralph-ified version of the game.

Calhoun lifts a specially rigged device. Vanellope is in the lead. As she rounds the curve, Calhoun takes aim.

A taffy lasso shoots from her weapon. Vanellope's tires squeal as she dodges it. Taffyta, in second place, isn't so lucky. Calhoun's next lasso snags her, bringing her kart to an abrupt stop.

"What the—" Taffyta says as karts zoom past her. Calhoun reloads.

"Look out!" Taffyta cries. "Someone's trying to catch us!"

Go to the NEXT PAGE.

You hear loud popping, accompanied by even louder shrieks. Excellent. The drivers must be passing Gene's popcorn machine.

You scramble down the tree so you can see how they handle the popcorn hail. You jump from gumdrop to gumdrop, trying to reach the spot ahead of the drivers.

You arrive in time to see three karts weaving through the onslaught of popcorn.

Wow, you think. *Those drivers are good.*

Go to the *NEXT PAGE*.

Next up—the rules change! Felix has been running around posting signs with new instructions. You can't wait to see how the drivers react to having **brand-new rules**!

You swing up into another candy cane tree. You shield your eyes from the bright lights and squint. Yup. You can just make out Felix in the distance. It looks like he has distributed all his signs.

You clamber back down and run along the track. You feel it rumble beneath your feet.

That's weird. Have you put on weight? Are you and your big bare feet making the ground tremble?

You glance back up to see a row of drivers heading straight toward you.

Uh-oh! You forgot that the first sign told the racers to drive backward.

Which means they're all heading straight for you!

Leap off the track on PAGE 127.

Calhoun punches your shoulder. "Well done, soldier. In fact, maybe you can help me redesign my game, too. Just to keep it spicy."

"Why, sure," you say.

"I bet some of the other games could use a little renewed energy," Felix says. "It was fun thinking up surprises."

Wow. You set out to make sure Vanellope wouldn't trade you in for a new, more exciting friend. Now there isn't just a super-excited Vanellope on the other side but a real sense of community among the other games and your fellow characters. That's what those in the game business call a **win**.

THE END.

You hang your head, feeling terrible. If Litwak can't find a new wheel, the game might end up being shut down. **Permanently.** And it will be all your fault!

You glance back out to the arcade. Several kids are now crowded around *Sugar Rush*.

"I'll try to find one on the Internet," a boy says, holding up his phone.

"Me too!" All the kids pull out their phones and start swiping and punching.

"I found one!" Swati cries.

Phew!

Go to the NEXT PAGE.

Swati hands her phone to Mr. Litwak. "See? **eBay** has a wheel, Mr. Litwak."

eBoy? What's that? you wonder. Then you shrug. As long as Mr. Litwak can get a steering wheel there, it doesn't matter *what* eBoy is.

"See," you say, "those kids have it under control."

Mr. Litwak adjusts his glasses and stares at the phone. His eyes grow wide. "Are you kidding me? How much? That's more than that game makes in a year." He hands the phone back to Swati. "I hate to say it, but my salvage guy is coming on Friday, and it might be time to sell *Sugar Rush* for parts."

"What?" Vanellope gasps.

Turn to PAGE 41.

You chortle to yourself. "She wants a challenge, I'll give her a challenge!"

You sneak into *Sugar Rush* to build a new track over Rocky Road and the Hot Fudge Bog, complete with some new signs to make sure Vanellope won't miss it. You finish just before Litwak's is about to open, and hide behind a hill of donuts near the final turn of the track, keeping your eyes peeled for the pack of racers. Sure, you need to get back to your own game any minute now, but first you want to see how this shakes out.

"There she is!" You clamp your hand over your mouth. You didn't mean to say that out loud! You don't want anyone to suspect you're here.

Vanellope is far ahead of all the other racers. Even from this distance you can see how bored she is. She's driving with one finger and barely glancing at the track.

You climb a nearby candy cane tree to watch. "Here she comes. She's going to love this. Right on time."

Turn to **PAGE 62**.

You turn slowly. Your eyes widen when you see the line of karts at the crest of the donut hill. Vanellope stands on the hood of her kart. She's rallying her drivers for . . . what? Are they going to come back and do the race? That would be great!

"Okay, to your places," you tell the Bad Guys. "Rein it in, though. You're too scary for—"

Your voice is drowned out by the powerful engines driving full speed down the hill.

Straight at you!

Freeze in fear on PAGE 197.

Vanellope gapes at you. "You did all this to make me happy?"

"Sure," you tell her. "I was afraid if you were bored with the game, maybe you were also bored with me."

"Never!" she assures you. "You *always* surprise me! Always keep me guessing. I'd never have guessed you could have pulled off a stunt like this!"

The drivers have all clambered out of their karts and come to join you and the Nicelanders. They all start gushing at once.

"Thanks, Ralph!" Minty says, her mint-green hair mussed.

"We never thought we could ever beat Vanellope. We were bored, too. It was frustrating," Taffyta tells you. She tugs at her chocolate-spattered candy-striped tights, but her big grin tells you she doesn't mind getting them messy.

"You leveled the playing field. It was *way* more fun," Crumbelina adds, tapping the icing brim of her hat.

Turn to PAGE 18.

You study the cityscape. Buildings of all different sizes rise from the main floor. Some have lots of connecting highways, and others have only one or two ways to reach them.

Two structures grab your attention. Both are castles! Very different castles. One is delicate and sparkly, with lots of turrets with colorful banners flying from them. The other looms like a medieval fortress, perched on a cliff.

Both have a steady flow of avatars streaming toward them, which means they must be popular.

So **where** should you go?

You can join the avatars heading for the sparkly castle by stepping onto the moving platform on PAGE 269.

Or hop aboard a high-speed train where the avatars approach the stone fortress on PAGE 86.

Or you can try to win the contest and go get that steering wheel on PAGE 30.

You watch as she stands and glitches down off the roof. She grows smaller and smaller, walking away from you.

"Okay," you call after her. "I'll meet you later?"

She doesn't even turn around.

You plop onto a pillow.

How did this happen? You tried to make the game more exciting for Vanellope so she wouldn't be bored and she would stay your friend forever. Instead, she's miserable and you're not even sure you're friends anymore.

You have to fix this. But **how**?

Should you figure out a way to get a replacement steering wheel to Litwak and his Family Fun Center? Turn to PAGE 73.

Or should you try to find a spot for Vanellope in another game? Turn to PAGE 187.

You get on your hands and knees. You're too big for the lanes in this baby-sized game. But you promised Vanellope you'd play along. So play you will.

You hear a little tinkling sound. The babies start to crawl. That must have been the signal to begin. You start crawling, too.

CRUNCH!

"Ow!"

You just crushed a baby rattle.

A baby starts to cry. *WHAP!* A dirty diaper lands in front of you. Gross.

You start crawling again. When you turn a corner, you come face to face with a baby. He takes one look at you and bursts into tears.

The ceiling opens above your head, and another dirty diaper drops in front of you. *WHAP!*

Ugh. Dirty diapers must be the penalties in this game! Double gross!

Go to the NEXT PAGE.

As far as you can tell, the players race the babies through the maze, collecting bottles, toys, and other baby-friendly items. But if a player makes a baby cry by breaking something or missing an item, *whammo-blammo*! It's dirty diaper time. You wonder how many dirty diapers can pile up before it's game over. . . .

You start to stand and knock a musical mobile to the ground. *WHAP!* This time the diaper slams onto your face!

You shudder and peel it off. "That's it!" you announce. "I'm done with this stupid game."

"Poor itty-bitty Walphie doesn't like the dirty didies?" Vanellope mocks.

"Oh, shush."

The babies are all crying now. It's deafening. Dirty diapers fly as you and Vanellope step over the barricades and knock things over, desperate to escape.

***Cover your head and race for the exit on** PAGE 188!*

"You think I should join *this* game?" Vanellope asks, surprised.

You're standing in front of the plug, about to go into *Hero's Duty.* That's the game Felix's wife, Calhoun, is in. Well, not just in—she's in charge! You've even played it. The cool thing about it is that if you destroy enough cy-bugs, you get a medal. And you love medals. So does Vanellope.

You gesture grandly to the game. "Welcome to *Hero's Duty.*"

Vanellope giggles. "You said 'doodie.'"

"That's the name of the game," you huff. "And don't make jokes like that around Calhoun. She takes this game *really* seriously."

"Sure." She gives you a mock salute. "Whatever you say, Officer Doodie-Head."

"Quit it," you say, trying not to laugh.

She points to the plug. "Is this where I go to do my doodie?"

"Cut it out!" you scold, even as you guffaw.

You and Vanellope collapse against each other, laughing. "Gotta go," she quips. "Doodie calls!"

"Ahem."

Uh-oh. Find out who is standing behind you on PAGE 38.

Vanellope tries a bunch of buttons on the control panel.
One shoots a laser beam that burns a hole in the hangar
wall. Another lifts the spaceship straight up. Then she
presses something that snaps the bubble shut over her.
Even through the shield, you can hear her cheering as she
zips out of the hangar.

You race outside and watch her zoom into the night sky.
Suddenly, dozens of aliens appear.

"Look out!" you cry, even though you know she can't
hear you.

The alien invaders send out volleys of light bursts.
Vanellope easily maneuvers around them. But they keep
coming.

"Fire on the aliens!" you shout.

Turn to PAGE 277.

You decide you better stay on task. You don't want to be stuck doing Ralph's laundry for a week!

"Steering wheel. Steering wheel, where could you be?" you say. You approach an avatar. "Hey, where do people go **shopping** in this place?"

But the avatar doesn't answer you. It doesn't even stop.

"Rude much?" you mutter.

A glamorous woman with hot-pink hair suddenly appears beside you. Her matching hot-pink dress is decorated with tiny pulsating lights. She holds a hot-pink smartphone. She looks as if she came from the future.

"You're looking for places to shop?" She holds the smartphone out so you can see the screen. "Have I got places to shop!"

A list of names scrolls down the screen.

Your eyes widen. "There must be a thousand places on that list," you sputter.

The woman smiles. "Oh, honey, I'd say hundreds of thousands!"

You sag with disappointment. "I'll never find the one I need."

Turn to PAGE 82.

You have to get the other drivers on board for your plan to work. So you wait until after the arcade closes that evening to suggest it.

You ask them all to meet you at the starting line. Once they've gathered, you begin your pitch. "I've been feeling like things have gotten kinda stale—"

Crumbelina cuts you off. "I'll say," she complains. "Those donuts on Donut Hill are definitely past their 'use by' date!"

"I meant the race," you explain. "*Us.*"

"Oh," Crumbelina says in a small voice.

"What do you have in mind?" Taffyta asks.

"Now, this would only be after hours," you say. You don't want any of them worrying about how changing the game would affect the players in the arcade. "I thought we could do a relay race. You know, race in teams."

You wait anxiously for their reaction. You're all so used to competing against each other that racing in teams is a new concept.

Find out what they think on PAGE 204.

"It's great that you have such faith in me," she says, "but how am I going to **contribute** to the game? It's not like I can smash things like you do."

"I am quite smashing, aren't I?" you say.

"What should I do?" Vanellope asks. "What's my role here?"

"Hmmmmm," you say.

You and Vanellope take a moment, trying to come up with ideas.

You snap your fingers. "I've got it!"

Turn to PAGE 40.

"Auditions are cancelled!" you bellow. You turn to Felix. "This is not going to work."

"Aw, please?" Zombie's head asks.

You stomp over to the building. "I can't believe Ralph left us in this fix!" you shout. You're so frustrated you smack the front door with your clipboard.

CRACK! You broke the window in the door. But you're so angry you don't even care.

"Go ahead, Felix," you holler. "Go ahead and fix that! And this! And this!" You furiously whack the building over and over again with your clipboard. Bricks fall, windows shatter, but still you keep at it. You're mad!

Go to the NEXT PAGE.

Finally, you're so exhausted all your anger drains away. You drop the clipboard and slump against the building.

Suddenly, you're surrounded. Felix shakes your hand. Sour Bill congratulates you. And Zombie gives you a half-hearted "Good job."

"Wh-what?" you stammer.

"That was an excellent performance!" Felix says. "You are the **best Bad Guy** for the job!"

"Me? A Bad Guy?" You're not sure how you feel about this. You just don't think of yourself that way. "Me," you repeat incredulously. "Bad."

"You'll start first thing tomorrow morning," Felix says.

Turn to PAGE 295.

You're dazed as you climb out of the kart. The other drivers swarm around you, peppering you with questions.

"Are you okay?"

"How's the car?"

"How'd you do that?"

You check yourself and then the kart. All is well. You grin. "I changed the fuel," you say. "And I have to say, it was *spectacular*!"

"Uh . . . you crashed," Taffyta reminds you.

"Oh, that," you scoff. "Just need to refine the formula."

"I want to try it, too!" Minty says. "You know, once you get the formula worked out."

"Sure thing!" you say.

The girls all clamor for the new fuel.

Then the quarter alert sounds through the game. "Oh, well, time to go to work," you say cheerfully. Once you've perfected the new fuel, *Sugar Rush* will be kicking into high gear.

Your experiment was a great success. Driving on Mentos power is going to require *all* your mad skills. But you'll only use the mint-and-cola fuel after hours. You don't think the human players will be able to handle the speed!

THE END.

"I think you're going to like this one," you tell Vanellope as you enter **Aliens Attack**. "It's right up your alley. It's not a race, but you get to drive!"

"I do?" Vanellope asks, brightening.

"Yup. But not a car—a spaceship."

Her eyes grow big. You can tell this game is going to be a hit with her.

You and Vanellope arrive inside a giant hangar filled with spaceships. They're pretty small. There's only enough room for the pilot.

"I'll just hang out here and watch," you tell Vanellope. You don't want to confess that the idea of flying around in outer space makes you queasy. But you know Vanellope can handle it.

You and Vanellope cross to a wall where space suits and helmets hang from pegs. "So, the object of this game is to shoot down the aliens," you tell Vanellope, handing her a helmet. "They're the ones in the green spaceships. All the good guys are in silver ones."

Vanellope buckles the helmet, then steps into the space suit you hold out for her.

Go to the NEXT PAGE.

You escort her down the row of identical spaceships. Each has a player number painted on its side. The tops are clear bubbles. When Vanellope jumps onto the wing of the spaceship identified as player one, the bubble pops open.

"Cool!" She jumps down into the seat and spins it. "Panoramic control panel!"

"Pan-o-*what*-ic?" you ask.

"It means it goes all the way around." She swivels in the seat a few more times. She grins. "Thanks, Ralph. I think I'm gonna like this one."

Grin back and then head to **PAGE 29.**

You and Vanellope freeze. You both put on serious expressions. You swallow hard, then turn around.

Yup. Just what you were afraid of. Calhoun stands behind you. And she doesn't look happy. In fact, she looks downright annoyed.

"Have you gotten the immature jokes out of your system?" she asks.

"Yes," you say.

"No," Vanellope says at the same time. "Did you hear the one about—"

You clamp your hand over Vanellope's mouth. "Vanellope here wants to try her hand at your game."

"Happy to see a new recruit." Calhoun suddenly stoops down to look Vanellope in the eye. "So long as the recruit knows how to follow orders, can face danger without even blinking, and doesn't give me any guff."

Uh-oh. Vanellope is definitely a guff-giver.

Go to the NEXT PAGE.

Calhoun straightens back up. She places her hands on her hips. "So, recruit. Are you ready to see what you're made of?"

You still have your hand over Vanellope's mouth, so you nod her head up and down for her.

"Yeowch!" you yelp, and release Vanellope. You frown at her. "Why'd you bite me?"

Vanellope smiles sweetly at you and then Calhoun. "Just practicing an escape technique. You know, in case I'm taken captive."

"Good thinking," Calhoun says with a sharp nod. "Follow me."

Follow her to *PAGE 154.*

"I'm strong," you say. "You're fast."

"Put those together and we've got a demolition derby going!" Vanellope says.

"Like you read my mind, kid," you tell her.

You and Vanellope dash around the side of the building. "Get ready for the wrecking-ist game ever!" you shout. You turn to Vanellope. "Ready?"

"Ready!"

You face the Nicelanders. "Ready?" you ask them.

"Ready!" they cry. They run into the building for their starting positions.

You nod at Vanellope.

"I'm gonna wreck it!" she shouts—just the way *you* do at the start of every game.

You start smashing windows. The Nicelanders poke their heads out and cry, "Fix it, Felix!" just like always.

And then Vanellope springs into action.

Turn to PAGE 90.

All the kids look crestfallen. Mr. Litwak turns his back and slowly trudges around the side of the machine.

You realize what he's about to do. "Litwak's gonna **unplug** your game! Go! Run, run, run!"

All the kart drivers dash away as fast as they can. You know if they get caught in the machine when it's unplugged they'll be trapped. And if Litwak is really going to sell the machine for parts, who knows *what* will happen to all those drivers.

Rush out of the game and into
Game Central Station on PAGE 178.

The stegosaurus steps carefully out of the remains of the shell. It looks up at you and Calhoun with huge eyes. You reach out and touch each of the plates sticking up along its spine. Seems like the best way to pet a dinosaur.

"It must belong in *Dino Park*," Calhoun surmises.

"You hear that, little guy?" you say to the baby dinosaur, who is happily chewing on your finger. "We can bring you home."

But when you go into *Dino Park*, the stegosaurus doesn't want to leave your side. Whenever you and Calhoun try to exit the game, the little fellow follows you. Then it sits down and cries.

"I've seen this sort of thing before," Ranger Mara says. She's in charge of the game. "You were the first thing the stego saw. So he thinks you and Calhoun are his **parents**."

You look at Calhoun. "What do you think? Should we add a dinosaur to our family?"

She looks at the stegosaurus stumbling over to you. "Oh, why not?" she says.

You pick up the baby dino and cuddle it. You hear a soft rumbling sound. "That must be how he purrs!" you say.

You and Calhoun take the baby stegosaurus home, delighted to have such an unusual pet.

You just wonder what the players will think when they see a dinosaur in the *Fix-It Felix, Jr.* game!

THE END.

"Shiny, shiny, shiny!" voices sing loudly.

"Shiny? What is going on? Where are you? Who's singing?"

Dishes dance around you. They're the ones singing. You're in a bright white room. All you see are the dishes.

"We're so clean, we're so clean!" the dishes sing.

"Where am I?" you ask. "And what have you done with Ralph?"

Sponges and dishcloths appear and twirl in front of you. *"Oh, if you use Shiny dishwashing soap, your dirty dishes won't make you mope!"* they sing.

"What? That's the stupidest rhyme I've ever heard."

The dishes grow brighter and brighter until their whiteness practically blinds you.

You squint against the dazzling whiteness. "How do I get out of here? I need to get back!"

"Buy Shiny and make your dishes happy!"

One by one the dishes hop into a stack. The top one stands up and a giant smiley face appears on it.

"Glad they shut up," you mutter. "Now I can think." You peer around the blank white room. "Now how do I—"

Suddenly, the music starts up again. The dishes jump down from the stack. *"Shiny, shiny, shiny,"* they sing.

You cover your ears. "Noooooooooooo! It's on a loop!"

Try to keep your wits and head for
PAGE 209.

"Hey, Vanellope!" Taffyta calls as she hops from one gumdrop to another. "You're going the wrong way! The arcade will open soon."

You pretend you don't hear her and keep going. You don't want the other drivers to know what you're up to. After all, your idea might be a total flop!

You pluck Mentos from the ground at the foot of the Mentos volcano and slip them into your pocket. Next— the beverage storage station. You whistle innocently as you stash a few bottles of cola in your hoodie, keeping a lookout for any passersby. Then you stroll along the path, nodding at Crumbelina and Swizzle as you awkwardly try to keep the hidden bottles in place. They give you quizzical looks but, luckily, don't stop. You hurry to your kart and hop into the driver's seat. Other drivers are hanging around the starting line, talking, making adjustments to their karts, and scarfing down breakfast. No one pays any attention to you. **Excellent.**

You drive the kart around the bend, just out of sight. "In go the Mentos," you say, plopping three candies into the tank. "And now . . ."

You freeze with the bottle of cola hovering above the fuel tank. You're pretty sure as soon as the cola hits the candy, the turbocharged fuel will surge into action.

You climb back into the kart and twist in the seat so you can reach the fuel tank.

"Three, two, one, blast off!" you cheer as you pour the carbonated beverage into the tank. The kart takes off like a rocket ship!

Blast off to **PAGE 279.**

You try to put an arm around Surge's shoulder, ready to guide him closer to the supply closet so that you can stash him inside for a bit, but you're knocked backward by a jolt.

"Yeow!" you yelp as you stumble and land on your backside. "You shocked me!"

Vanellope frowns, then reaches out to give Surge a tentative poke. She's promptly thrown back as well.

"What gives, dude?" she asks, rubbing her hand gingerly.

"I'd ask you the same thing," Surge says, glaring at you both. "Whatever it is, it seems like it's against the rules."

Turn to **PAGE 110**.

"I don't know," Ralph says reluctantly. He rubs the back of his thick neck. "It's probably pretty easy to get lost out there. Wouldn't want you to not be able to find your way back."

"Don't worry about me," you assure him. "You're the one who'll probably get lost."

"Am not."

"Are too."

"Am not."

"Are too."

"Are too what?" Ralph asks.

You pause, trying to remember what you were talking about.

Oh, right!

Should you split up? Go to PAGE 50.

Or should you stay together on PAGE 250?

First thing you have to do is go into the new **Wi-Fi** socket. Once you get to the Internet, you'll find that eBoy place and snag yourself one *Sugar Rush* steering wheel.

You go to Game Central Station and head for the marquee that reads WI-FI in big, bright letters. You're almost there when you see something that makes your stomach sink.

Surge Protector did as he said he would. He blocked the plug with a mass of caution tape. You're going to have to get around the tape and into the plug without alerting Surge Protector.

That's not going to be easy. Surge Protector is patrolling the area. But you were prepared for this. You pull a brick from your game out of one of your overalls' many pockets and toss it. It skitters across the floor.

Good. Surge Protector is on it. He rushes to see what made the racket. You have to give the guy credit—he takes his job *very* seriously.

You sneak up to the socket and study it.

Go to the NEXT PAGE.

You lift the tape and step under it, making your way into the plug slowly and cautiously.

With a careful glance over your shoulder, you check to make sure Surge Protector hasn't seen you. When you see that he hasn't, you can't quite believe it. That was almost too easy. You take off at a run, eager to get your mission underway.

But you get a little too excited. Your feet get tangled up underneath you and you trip, careening indelicately into the side of the plug.

You hear a cracking sound. Uh-oh. That can't be good.

You look up to see the plug is damaged. With a flicker, the marquee light goes out.

Well, your name *is* Wreck-It Ralph. And that's what you're going to tell Surge Protector. You can't go against your nature. You just gotta be you in . . .

 *THE END.*

Up ahead are Minty and Crumbelina, looking exactly the way they do in your *Sugar Rush*. And standing with them is none other than . . . *you*! Well, the **other** you. In the whole princess getup. No wonder Taffyta was surprised by your outfit.

Taffyta's mouth drops open and she takes a step away from you. "If you're here," she says, pointing a shaky finger at you, "then who's that over there?" She turns and points the shaky finger toward the other Vanellope.

"It's kind of a long story," you say.

Explain it to them all on PAGE 296.

"We'll double our chances by splitting up," you say.

"All righty then," Ralph replies reluctantly.

"Ooooh, I have an idea!" you say. "Let's make this in-ter-est-ing."

"Are you suggesting what I think you're suggesting?" Ralph says with a grin.

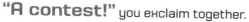

"A contest!" you exclaim together.

"Does the winner get a medal?" Ralph asks eagerly.

"Sure," you tell him. You know how much Ralph loves medals. "Here's how it will go: whoever gets the steering wheel first, go back to Game Central Station immediately. We have to make sure Litwak doesn't get rid of *Sugar Rush.*"

"Absotively," Ralph says with a sharp nod. He smirks. "And the loser has to do the winner's laundry for a week."

You eye Ralph. Washing those overalls alone could take a week. But you're confident it won't come to that. You hold out your hand. "Deal."

"Deal," Ralph says, giving your hand a firm pump. "Wait— the winner needs to let the loser know they have the wheel. Otherwise the loser might stay in here forever. . . ."

"Hmm. That's a puzzler." You and Ralph sit down to think. "There must be some way to get a message to somebody in the Internet."

Go to the NEXT PAGE.

"**Message?**" A woman driving a small vehicle screeches to a stop in front of you and Ralph. An envelope is painted on the side of the mini truck. "Do you have an e-mail message for me to deliver?"

"Uh, not right now," Vanellope says.

"Maybe later," Ralph adds.

"So how do we do that?" you ask.

"Just flag one of us down," the woman says. "There are about a million of us traveling through all corners of the Internet just to get messages through!"

"Wow," you say. "Impressive."

"You'd think people would say thank you once in a while," the woman grouses.

"Thank you," you and Ralph chime together.

She beams. "You are very welcome! Ta-ta!"

You watch as she drives away. "So that problem is solved. Just be on the lookout for one of those e-mail deliverers for a note from me."

"*You* be on the lookout," Ralph counters. "Since *I'll* be sending *you* the message that I found that wheel first!"

You watch Ralph hop on board a sleek train. You wonder where it's headed. Probably somewhere completely awesome. Just like everywhere in this amazing place.

You know you need to find your steering wheel, but how can you pass up a chance to explore? Call it a reconnaissance mission. Besides, Surge Protector might figure out a way to keep you and Ralph out after this. This could be your only opportunity.

But what do you want to check out?

Try to decide on **PAGE 24.**

The drivers leap out of their karts, banging into one another as they dash around, desperate to escape. You watch as the **Bad Guys** chase them up and over the donut hill.

Once the drivers have dropped down on the other side, the Bad Guys trudge back to you.

"That was fun!" Zombie says, huffing a bit from the exertion.

But was it fun for the drivers? Did you and the Bad Guys go too far?

Go to the *NEXT PAGE.*

The Bad Guys cheer and give each other high fives. You rub the back of your neck, thinking.

"Maybe we should tone it down a little," you say. "I want to make the game more challenging. Not **traumatic**."

"But we're Bad Guys," Cyborg protests. "We've got to stay true to ourselves."

"Let me be me!" Cycloptopus adds, his giant eye gazing at you imploringly.

You're starting to think this might not have been your best idea. The drivers were really scared. Even Vanellope ran away over that hill.

Should you go and apologize? Coax them out from wherever they're hiding?

Go to the NEXT PAGE.

You turn and see that the Bad Guys have already scattered. They're spread across the game doing what Bad Guys do best. Cyborg smashes gumdrops. Zombie chops down candy cane trees with his hatchets. Sorceress curdles buttercream-frosting meadows with a flick of her blue fingers.

This **isn't** what you had in mind. You don't want them to destroy the game! Your plan was for them to jump out and surprise the racers as they drove around the track.

"Hey!" You wave your hands to get their attention. "Stop. We need to—"

A sound behind you drowns you out.

Vrooom, vrooom, vrooom!

You know that sound: a dozen or more engines revving up.

Turn to PAGE 22.

You don't want to risk wasting any more time. The *Sugar Rush* drivers are counting on you. You point at the picture of your game.

KnowsMore taps some keys on his keyboard. "All righty then," he says. "This is being sold over at eBay. They have a number of replacement parts, including your steering wheel."

"We found it!" you cheer.

"How do we find this bay?" Ralph asks "Do we need to take a boat?"

"It's not that kind of bay," KnowsMore says.

"Then why is 'bay' in its title?" Ralph presses.

"C'mon, Ralph," you say, tugging on his hand. You know he can get caught up in these kinds of conversations. "Our steering wheel is a'waitin'"

KnowsMore looks relieved to get Ralph to stop asking questions he doesn't have answers for. "All you have to do is tap on the screen," he instructs you and Ralph. "You will be taken directly to your destination."

"Ready?"

"Ready!"

Then go to PAGE 150!

"First round," the announcer continues. "Match the moves of our resident dancer, Rockin' Roger!"

A screen descends. A guy in a sequined suit appears. He gives everyone a huge smile and a double thumbs-up. You notice there are now screens all around the club. *Makes sense,* you think. No matter where you are on the dance floor, you can see Rockin' Roger's moves. This could be fun! You never tried dancing before.

"You might want to stay up there, kid," you tell Vanellope, still perched on your shoulder. "It's pretty crowded down here. Wouldn't want you to get stepped on!"

"**Owww!**" A man next to you grabs his foot and hops around. "Watch where you're going, you big oaf."

"Sorry!" you tell him.

"You're right," Vanellope says, laughing. "It's safer up here. Away from your size-twenty-dozen feet!"

"On the count of three!" the announcer booms.

All around you, the contestants move into position. Some are dancing with partners, others solo. They all look serious. "One! Two! . . ."

Get your best moves ready, then leap like a ballet dancer to PAGE 137.

You find Vanellope in the dump on your pile of bricks.

"Hey, kid!" you shout.

"Ralph!" She startles. "What is wrong with you?" she asks, rubbing the sleep from her eyes.

"Start churning butter and put on your church shoes, little sister, 'cause we're about to blast off!" you say.

She looks at you, confused. "What are you even talking about?"

"We're going to the Internet," you say with a shrug.

"What?"

"Yeah," you continue, "to find the part to fix your game."

She jumps up.

"Really?" she asks. "Oh my gosh! Really?!"

"Yeah, I probably should have just said, 'We're going to the Internet.' We're going to the Internet! C'mon!"

You turn to take off, and Vanellope follows you.

Get going to PAGE 101.

"Follow my lead," you tell her.

She gives you a salute. "Lead on, fearless leader."

You and Vanellope stroll nonchalantly over to the socket wall. "Hey, there, buddy," you greet Surge Protector. **"How's it goin'?"**

He glances up from his clipboard. "Something I can do for you?"

"We don't spend enough quality time together," Vanellope says.

"Exactly," you say with a broad smile. "We were just saying that, weren't we, kid? That we need to get to know Surge better."

Surge narrows his eyes and peers at you—suspiciously.

You'd better make your move before he's on to you and you lose your chance.

Turn to **PAGE 45**.

There are just too many aliens now. You can't watch!

You cover your eyes. You hear an explosion.

Oh, no! If Vanellope dies outside her game, she won't regenerate! Why didn't you think of that when you brought her into such a dangerous place? *Worst idea ever!* you scold yourself.

You peek through your fingers and see Vanellope's ship in pieces. "Thank goodness for parachutes," you murmur as you watch Vanellope slowly drift to the ground.

You race over to her. "Why didn't you fight the aliens?" you demand as she undoes the parachute straps. "That's how you win the game."

Vanellope shrugs. "Flying that ship was a lot more fun than just punching the 'blast' button."

"Do you want to go again?" you ask.

"Nah," Vanellope says. "The game ends too quick."

"Well, yeah, if you don't play it right."

"The flying part was fun," she admits, "but I'm out there all on my own. I like having all the *Sugar Rush* drivers there, too. In this game it's just me versus the aliens. So good effort, pal o' mine, but I don't think this game is for me."

Fair enough. Go back to PAGE 189 *and choose another game for her to try.*

You give Ralph an appreciative nod, then continue. "Specifically, we are looking for the steering wheel from the classic arcade game *Sugar Rush*."

KnowsMore's face is turning blue and he begins gesturing wildly.

"You can let him go now, Ralph. I'm done."

"You got that?" Ralph says, still covering KnowsMore's mouth. "Steering wheel. *Sugar Rush*."

KnowsMore nods frantically. You can tell it's not just from needing to breathe. He's full of answers itching to get out. Ralph releases him.

KnowsMore takes in a huge breath, then words tumble out of him. "*Sugar Rush*. Steering wheel. Got it." Instantly, several images of your game pop up on the counter in front of you. In the corner of each image is an insert: a close-up of the steering wheel.

"Um . . . Why don't they look identical?" Ralph asks, scratching his head.

KnowsMore opens his mouth, then shuts it again. "Is it okay if I answer that?" he asks tentatively.

"Please do," you say. You gesture extravagantly, indicating you are giving him permission to speak. Being a princess, you've learned a few fancy moves.

Go to the NEXT PAGE.

KnowsMore is so thrilled to be allowed to unleash his knowledge, facts and figures tumble out of him. All of which add up to this: there are **five** other versions of *Sugar Rush* out there!

"Who knew?" you say. You're surprised but pleased.

"Not us, that's for sure," Ralph says.

You and Ralph study the different games.

"Do you know which one is yours?" Ralph asks.

You do. But now you wonder if there's a way to play those other versions of *Sugar Rush*.

Do you point to the correct Sugar Rush *and go get that steering wheel on* PAGE 55?

Or do you try to figure out a way to play each of those variations of Sugar Rush *on* PAGE 203?

Your grin practically consumes your face as she barrels down the track, passing your homemade signs. Just as you'd hoped she would, Vanellope follows them to your new track—a detour made just for her. And from the way she's driving, she loves it!

"Thank you, Ralph!" she shouts gleefully as she speeds through the turns.

But then she starts to struggle against the wheel.

Your grin starts shrinking. "Uh-oh," you murmur as you watch her try to regain control of the kart. It's swerving and zigzagging and—

Go to the NEXT PAGE.

She misses a turn and careens off the road and into a ditch.

This didn't go exactly how you'd planned. . . .

You jump down from the candy cane tree and rush over to her.

"Kid, are you okay?" you ask. Her kart is stuck in a chocolate puddle.

"Ohmygosh, that was so much fun!" she exclaims. "What an amazing track! Thank you, thank you, thank you!"

"Vanellope, get up here!" someone calls from the top of the donut hill. It's Taffyta, another driver. "We have a situation."

You help Vanellope out of the kart. Thankfully, she's not hurt. You both join Taffyta at the crest of the hill. Immediately, you see the problem: the *Sugar Rush* steering wheel is broken!

"What did you do, Ralph?" Taffyta asks.

Vanellope jumps in before you can answer, though. "He was just trying to make the game more exciting. Leave him alone."

"Yeah," you chime in. "Why don't you relax, Taffyta? Litwak'll fix it."

Turn to PAGE 130.

"Are you searching for something?" A small man wearing a headset and holding a keyboard steps up to you.

"Ignore him!" A woman drives up on a cart. When she hops out, you see she was sitting on an enormous directory. You notice a logo with a magnifying glass is painted across the side of the cart.

"No no no no!" A guy carrying a search box sign pushes his way to you and Vanellope.

"Back off!" KnowsMore shouts. "They came to ask for *my* help!"

They all ignore him and continue to press forward.

Vanellope glitches up to your shoulder to avoid being crushed. "Who are they?"

KnowsMore sighs. "Other search engines."

"You mean they each have a different way to look for something?" Vanellope asks.

"Yes," KnowsMore admits. "And they all believe they're the best. Incorrectly, of course," he adds. "Everyone knows *I* have the most powerful search tools in all of the Internet."

Go to the NEXT PAGE.

"Oh, yeah?" The search engine with the headset takes a menacing step toward KnowsMore's counter.

"No way!" says the woman who came in on the cart.

"My results come in so fast—"

"I have access to—"

They're all shouting over each other.

Uh-oh. It looks like a fight is about to break out.

Turn to PAGE 289.

YOU ARE NOW FIX-IT FELIX, JR.

YOU WONDER WHAT **HIJINKS** Ralph and Vanellope are going to get up to in that Internet place. You chuckle to yourself. "Those netizens don't know what they're in for!"

For now, *Sugar Rush*'s plug has been pulled. But you have faith that those two rascals will do their gosh-darnedest to find that replacement wheel. The arcade isn't open tomorrow, so that gives them time to take care of that bit of business. Also, with the newfangled Wi-Fi thingamabob and the uncertainty about the future of *Sugar Rush*, everyone's feeling a bit topsy-turvy. It's for the best that everyone will have a day off. Who knows what might result from these brand-new changes? But you're **Fix-It Felix, Jr.**, so if anything is amiss, you are determined to fix it.

Turn to **PAGE 87**.

You stroll through Game Central Station, whistling. You pass one of the newer games brought in to please the younger set: **Baby Bonanza**. The nanny in charge of the game stands beside the plug. She looks exhausted. Her hair is mussed, there's baby formula spattered across her uniform, and her eyes are shut as if she's asleep standing up. You hear a baby start to cry in the game above her.

"Pardon me," you say as you approach her. "But I do believe one of your charges needs attention."

Her eyes open and she sighs. "Not as much as I need a night off."

Before you can respond, an adorable puppy races up to you. It plants its front paws on your legs, just begging for you to pet it. "Where'd you come from, little cutie?" you say, scratching it behind its ears.

"There's a pet shop game nearby," Miss Nanny says. "It must have gotten out somehow."

You glance around and your eyes land on a strange sight. A large egg sits on the floor near a bench.

Here are three things that need attention. A stray puppy. A stranded egg. And a super-tired nanny. Your help is needed, but you can't be in three places at once!

Will you take care of the puppy on
PAGE 285?

Find out where the egg belongs on
PAGE 182?

Or go into **Baby Bonanza** *so Miss Nanny can have the night off on* **PAGE 253**?

Cy-bugs swarm everywhere. You hear lasers pinging all around you. Vanellope runs a few steps, then trips over her pant leg. You rush to help her up, but she's already on her feet. She takes aim and shoots her laser.

The soldier in front of her grabs his butt and yelps. She missed the bug but clipped the soldier!

"Oops," Vanellope says. She wrestles her visor around. "This stupid face mask got in my way. I couldn't aim properly."

Calhoun appears beside you. "I applaud your enthusiasm, cadet. But I don't think you're cut out for this."

"I agree," Vanellope says. "This one isn't for me."

Well, it was worth a shot.

Turn to PAGE 189 *and choose another game.*

"Wow," you say, gazing around. "It's a lot smaller in here than in my *Sugar Rush*." Something tickles your nose and you sneeze. "A lot dustier, too."

You wander the familiar but not familiar landscape. You note the differences and the similarities. "Oooh, their clouds are cotton candy, not marshmallows," you say. "I think I'm going to suggest that. But their chocolate pond is much too shallow."

You notice a girl arriving at the top of the donut hill. She looks exactly like Taffyta in your game, but with red hair instead of blond.

She spots you and does a double take. "Princess Vanny, what are you wearing?" she asks. She jogs down the donuts to meet you.

You glance down at yourself. You're in your usual attire: green hoodie, short black skirt, striped tights, and high-tops. "Um, I'm wearing my clothes?"

"Where's your tiara?" she asks, pointing to your head. "Your beautiful sparkly gown with the five petticoats?"

"Five petticoats?" You snort. "It would be awfully hard to drive wearing five petticoats."

Taffyta sighs. "That's probably true. But it's not like we've been doing much driving."

"What?" You're shocked.

Turn to **PAGE 191.**

"Come on, Ralph," you say. "Let's get a move on. Time's a'wasting."

"Have fun," the security officer says. "And don't let the pop-ups lead you astray." He strolls away. "You, there!" you hear him shout. "What do you plan to do with those cookies?"

"I guess he's the Surge Protector type," Ralph comments.

"I'm thinking, Ralph . . ."

"Never a good idea," he teases.

You ignore the remark and continue. "Maybe we should **split up**," you suggest as you gaze at the vastness before you. "Cover more territory that way."

Turn to **PAGE 46**.

"You're probably wondering why I gathered you all here," you tell the assembled **Nicelanders**. You're in Gene's penthouse in your *Fix It Felix, Jr.* game.

"You know how much Vanellope means to me," you say. "So, I'd really appreciate it if you'd help me make her happy."

"You can count on us!" Felix declares. "Am I right, Nicelanders?"

The Nicelanders shuffle their feet, look down, and generally pretend they didn't hear Felix.

Felix frowns. You do, too.

He steps up beside you. "I know that Vanellope and Ralph may have played some pranks on you," he says, "but I think we can all agree they're lovable scamps."

Gene clears his throat, then glances away.

"Um . . . yes . . . sure," a woman in the corner says.

This isn't going very well.

Go to the **NEXT PAGE.**

Felix plants his hands on his hips and shakes his head. "Nicelanders! I'm ashamed of you. We're supposed to be *nice*. That means we pitch in when someone in our community asks us to."

Wow. He's really taking them to task. You didn't know Felix had it in him.

He turns to you. "I'm happy to volunteer. Just tell me what you want me to do."

"What did you just volunteer for?" someone calls out.

It's Calhoun, Felix's wife. She's an intense military type. She battles cy-bugs in her game, *Hero's Duty*. She and Felix met when you and Vanellope met.

You're not sure how she's going to react to Felix's offer to help you.

"Uh, here's my idea," you say, hoping Calhoun doesn't nix the deal. "Vanellope is feeling a bit, well, bored. I thought if we went in and added a few surprises to her game, it might be more challenging. You know, keep things more interesting."

"I'm in," Calhoun says immediately, to your surprise. "I could use some extra training in handling the unexpected. Keeps me sharp."

You have no doubt she'll add a certain, er, challenge to *Sugar Rush*.

"Glad we'll be trying something new together, sweetums," Felix tells her.

"I suppose I can lend a hand," Gene says, straightening his bow tie.

"Great!" You clap your hands. "Meet me at *Sugar Rush* in ten!"

Turn to PAGE 243.

Just when my life is perfect, you think sadly, *I go and wreck it. I suppose I shouldn't be surprised. After all, I'm Wreck-It Ralph. Can't escape destiny.* You let out a long, sad sigh.

You shake your head, trying to shake off your mood. You're no quitter! You clap your huge hands on your knees and stand up. Things are going to change! They changed before; they can change again.

What did those kids in the arcade say? They found the *Sugar Rush* steering wheel over in that new Internet place. Somewhere called Oh-Boy or E-Bee or eBoy or something. It's the only thing you can think of that will make Vanellope happy. So that's what you're going to do. You're going to find that place and get a new steering wheel for *Sugar Rush.* That will put everything right again.

Tell Vanellope what you're going to do on PAGE 57.

Don't tell Vanellope on PAGE 47.

One problem: the plug is covered in caution tape. You don't have a lot of time. "Let's smash our way through it," you suggest, holding up your huge hammer-like hands.

"Not so fast, Smasher Supreme," Vanellope says. "Wrecking isn't always the answer."

You lower your hand. You can't help pouting a little, even though you know she's right.

She steps forward and studies the plug carefully. **"Easy-peasy!"** she exclaims. "Let's just go around it."

You lift the caution tape up high enough that she can slip under, then you follow behind her. When you're through, you slap each other high fives.

"And now . . . into the Internet!" you announce.

Turn to **PAGE 286**.

You can't stay away from your game too long, so it would probably be a good idea to split up. There are so many different ways to search!

"Okay, Ralph, I'll check out what that guy has to offer!" Vanellope says. She points at the giant search box sign.

He hurries over to you and Vanellope. "At your service. You've made the right choice."

Vanellope glitches off your shoulder. The search engine slips his arm through hers and leads her quickly away. The other two search engines rush toward you.

"Nope!" you tell them. You hold out your massive hand to stop them. "I'm going with the little college guy."

They grumble, but the woman drives off in her cart, and the man with the headset strides away.

KnowsMore adjusts his cap, bringing the little tassel to the front. "Now then," he says. "Would you like to tell me your keywords?"

You pat your pockets. "Um, I seem to have left my keys at home."

KnowsMore looks confused.

Go to the NEXT PAGE.

"What is it you are searching for?" KnowsMore prompts. "And where would you like to search?"

You think back to the kids in the arcade. They found a *Sugar Rush* steering wheel in the Internet. Which is why you're here now. But where? They said the place was amazing. That's a start, right?

"Okay, we—" You look around and remember Vanellope has already rushed to who knows where. "That is, *I* am looking for this place that sells things."

A blank window opens up on the counter in front of you. KnowsMore's fingers hover over a keyboard.

"I hear it's amaz—"

You watch, intrigued, as the letters *a, m, a,* and *z* appear in the window as KnowsMore types. But instead of completing the word with the letters *i, n,* and *g,* the letters *o* and *n* appear.

"'Amazon'?" you read. You're instantly encapsulated in a pod and whisked away.

"How am I going to find a steering wheel in a jungle?" you cry.

Arrive at your destination on **PAGE 118.**

You stroll through collections of pictures, all shapes and sizes. Pictures of everything! Flowers, people, cats and dogs, stars, planets, trees, shoes, and lots and lots of food.

"There must be rules for the game," you mutter. "I just have to figure them out."

You grab a few small pictures and arrange them to form a big rectangle. "If you rearrange the little pictures, do they make a big picture?" You step back and study the result. "That doesn't look like much."

You find a few more little pictures. You place them together, making a triangle by laying one on its side to form the tip.

"Nope. That's just confusing."

You continue walking among the photos, hoping you'll figure out how to play the game.

Ponder the rules on your way to
PAGE 199.

You find yourself on another loading platform, gazing out over the massive islands of the Internet. Lights flash on and off, signs whirl and twirl, and netizens bustle around. You have no idea where to try next.

You sigh. *That Instagram game had a lot of pictures of friends,* you think. Will Vanellope still be your friend if her game is unplugged forever?

Even more important—will you ever find her in this vast maze? Everything seems to lead to everywhere all at once! How does anyone ever find their way around?

You plop down on a guardrail and hang your head. "What if I never find her again?"

"Find who?" someone asks above you.

You glance up to see a tall striking woman. Her short black hair swoops over one eye. With her snazzy white dress and turquoise dangly earrings, she looks fancy—and important.

"You can find anything you want!" she tells you. "You just have to know how to look. And do I know how!"

You slide away from her. "Are you one of those search engines?"

She laughs, "I am *so* much better. Search engines seek *me* out to find out what's going on!"

You perk up. You have a feeling she's just the person to help you find Vanellope *and* the steering wheel.

Turn to PAGE 257.

She spins you around, and you walk with her to an entire arena of screens. Each displays something different. "I love this place!" she gushes as she guides you into a seat. "They have the best **GIFs** and **memes**!"

"The best whats and the whats?"

She gapes at you. "Where have you been living? Under a rock?"

"On a pile of bricks in a dump, actually."

She bursts out laughing. "I like you. You're so . . . retro!"

"Well, yeah, my game is considered—"

She chucks you under the chin. "Maybe we should get you up to speed on a few things, or your head is going to explode."

"Oh, my head doesn't do that," you tell her. "You must be thinking of a different game."

She looks perplexed a moment, but then jumps up from her seat. "Oooh, look at that one!" She grabs your hand and drags you over to one of the screens. It's playing a movie of a puppy on a skateboard. But the movie is only about five seconds long. Then it repeats. Over and over.

Yesss giggles. "I just could watch that forever. Oh, look at that one!"

Dash to the next GIF on the NEXT PAGE.

Yesss rushes from screen to screen, dragging you along with her. You wonder why there are even seats in the arena, since no one seems to stay still in this place. Lots of people dash from one screen to another.

"Goat yoga! A cat playing the piano! A snowboarder's trick! Oooh, the latest hit from Jenny Flashdrive! Gotta respect the girl power!" Yesss tosses **hearts** at each of the mini movies.

She's making you dizzy. "But what about finding my friend?" you ask. You drop into a seat, hoping she'll do the same thing.

And you thought Vanellope was hard to keep up with!

Go to the NEXT PAGE.

She sits beside you. "Your friend?" she asks. "Is that what you're looking for? One of your friends?"

"Yes. My friend Vanellope. Also, a steering wheel," you add before she can hurry on to another topic.

"Have you consulted your friends list?" she suggests. "Maybe she checked in somewhere."

"I don't have a list," you say. "I can remember them without writing down their names."

She stares at you. "Really?" she says, incredulous. "I can barely keep track of my ten million, three hundred forty-five thousand, nine hundred eighty-two friends. And I update my list all the time."

Turn to **PAGE 96.**

"Don't fret!" the woman says. "Yesss has the line on all things Internet."

You scrunch your eyebrows together. "Yesss?" You repeat. "Oookay. Who are you?"

She laughs. "I'm the head of algorithm."

You nod, but you have no idea what that is. "What does that mean?" you ask.

"It means I know everything about everything that goes on here. I've got my fingers—and my codes—in all of it. I can—"

You cut her off. You have a feeling she could go on awhile. "Can you help me find a steering wheel?"

She pauses, her mouth open. Then she frowns. "I haven't heard anything about steering wheels trending."

"I don't care if they're trending," you snap. "I just need one!"

Turn to **PAGE 246**.

"First I'll post a listing on all the selling sites with interested buyers!" she says. "That way if anyone has one, they'll reach out directly to let us know. Then we'll do our own search. We'll use keywords, descriptors, oooh, anything we can think of to cast the widest net."

You have no idea what she's talking about, but you don't want to interrupt to ask. She's far too busy. She's tapping on her eyeglasses and typing furiously on a phone that she seems to have conjured out of thin air. All around her screens are popping up. It's dizzying.

"How can you keep track of all that?" you ask, your eyes darting from screen to screen to screen.

She gives you a wink. "Multitasking is my middle name, big guy."

Try to keep up on PAGE 247.

You and Felix scribble notes as Zombie and Sour Bill go through their paces.

"Dig deep," Felix coaches Sour Bill. He hasn't been able to smash anything since that first window. "You were so bad before. Try again."

"I can't," Sour Bill huffs. His green face is turning red with exertion.

You notice Zombie has made some progress. A few windows on his side have been smashed. You spot him crawling up to the next level. That's when you realize—with each item he breaks, one of his body parts falls off!

"I never realized Zombie was so fragile," you say to Felix.

Turn to PAGE 174.

This Internet place is wearing you out. The constant movement, the noise, the crowds, the confusion. You need a break. So you decide to let Yesss take over the search for the steering wheel and Vanellope. You'll just take a little nap.

But it's important to keep going, right? So go to PAGE 102, where you will become . . .

You hop a packed train. It's mostly populated by **avatars**—those representatives of humans out in the world. It must be a big game, you realize with excitement, if this many people are playing it.

The train leaves the city and chugs through a deep forest. When you emerge on the other side, the train travels through flower-filled, sun-drenched meadows. You shade your eyes to peer at the massive castle growing even larger the closer you get. It looks well fortified, and you spot knights with lances standing watch among the turrets.

The train stops in a shaded area. The station is well disguised—you barely notice it once you get out. Avatars pile out in a rush. You're amazed to see them transform in front of you. Some are putting on armor; some sprout wings. A few grow taller, some become tiny—and a few even turn into animals!

Turn to PAGE 244.

You know there are some Nicelanders who were surprised when you and your lovely bride tied the knot. The two of you really are quite different. She's from *Hero's Duty*, a fully animated, gorgeously rendered, high-octane, high-energy game. You're from an old-school eight-bit game.

She towers over you. She destroys dangerous cy-bugs. You fix what Ralph wrecks using the magic hammer your father passed on to you, as his father passed it on to him. She's tougher than beef jerky; you're a bit on the soft and squishy side. But no one can deny how much you love each other.

Maybe, you muse, *it's our differences that make our marriage so strong.*

Go to **PAGE 67**.

"Does this belong to you?" Mr. Carlyle, who runs the snack shop, approaches you carrying the puppy.

The puppy wriggles with delight and keeps trying to lick Mr. Carlyle's nose. Mr. Carlyle doesn't look amused. He dumps the puppy into your arms.

"Please keep your animal under control," Mr. Carlyle says. "Fourteen ham sandwiches were gone before I noticed he was eating them!"

"I'm so sorry," you say, placing the puppy on the floor. He instantly wraps the leash around your legs. "And of course I'll pay for those sandwiches."

"Will you pay for my slippers, too?" Sorceress stalks over to you. She looks mad. "I just bought new slippers and set them on the bench beside me. Next thing I know, your little beast had snagged one and chewed it all up!" She waves the mangled fluffy slipper at you.

"Oh, dear." You sigh. You haven't done a very good job of fixing this situation.

Turn to **PAGE 225.**

All around you, Bad Guys are shouting, screaming, and calling for help. The drivers of *Sugar Rush* race around them, sending them up trees, making them duck for cover, and generally terrorizing them.

You watch, amazed, as the drivers perform tricks and stunts you've never seen before. They drive up and over obstacles, balance on just two wheels, and practically fly. The racers drive as well backward as they do forward, making it impossible for the Bad Guys to predict which direction they'll come from!

"**Oh my . . .**" is all you can say.

The Bad Guys run terrified out of the game.

Well, that was a surprise.

Turn to **PAGE 148.**

Vanellope zips around the building wreaking havoc. She eats the pies before Felix can collect them. After you break a brick, she tosses the pieces around, making it harder for Felix to fix them. She startles the Nicelanders when they peek out their windows.

By the end of the game, Felix is huffing and puffing. And he had to reset many more times than he usually does before getting his medal.

Gene comes up to you and Vanellope and shakes your hands. "That was one exciting game," he says.

"Well, I must admit, you certainly put me through my paces," Felix says.

"Hope that's okay," you say. It took Felix a lot longer to win this game. In fact, you and Vanellope kept him on level two for so long, you wondered if he'd ever make it all the way through the game! You hope it doesn't trouble him.

"Oh, I loved it," he assures you. "The wife thinks I should be getting more exercise. With this little scamp throwing me for a loop, I'll keep nice and fit."

You and Vanellope grin at each other. You found a perfect solution for her.

Just one problem: what are the kids in the arcade going to think when they see Vanellope chasing Felix?

Oh, well. You suppose as long as it's fun, it will all work out in . . .

THE END.

Surge throws up his hands. "I have no idea! There has never been a circuit overload since we Protectors started patrolling." He sighs and slumps to the floor. You've never seen him like this. Mad, annoyed, irritated, and full of himself, sure. But never sad, never distraught. You feel terrible.

You can tell Vanellope feels the same way. She plops onto the floor beside him. "We'll help you fix it," she promises.

Another sigh. "You can't. It all has to be taken care of from the outside."

"Then we'll wait with you until the lights come back on," you tell Surge Protector. You join him and Vanellope on the floor. "And we'll explain to everyone it was our fault."

"Thanks," he murmurs.

Go to the NEXT PAGE.

"You know, there's actually a silver lining," you tell him, trying to get him to see the bright side. Which may be a tall order, since there's nothing bright in the darkness surrounding you.

"Yeah?" Surge Protector says sullenly. "What's that?"

"Until now, we thought of you as just some guy who was a little too into rules. You know, a spoilsport who never wanted us to have any fun. But now I understand how important you are."

"Me too," Vanellope says. "It's like you're . . . *crucial*!"

"Yeah," you say. "Critically important."

You can tell by the way he's sitting up a little straighter that you're making him feel better.

"And we are going to let everyone know that what you do is as important to them as it is to you," you promise. "And that we should get a little bit better at following the rules."

"A *little* bit," Vanellope emphasizes.

"Thank you," Surge says. "That means a lot."

And you know what, to your surprise, you actually mean what you said!

So there is a happily ever after in . . .

THE END.

"What would be the point of racing?" Taffyta asks. "If no one is playing the game?"

You stare at her. "For excitement! For **fun**! Keep up your skills! Develop new skills."

"I guess we've gotten a bit lazy," Princess Vanny confesses. "With no actual players, we just let things slide."

"Time for that to change," you declare. "Let's race now!"

Your enthusiasm is contagious. The girls cheer.

"It's just you four?" you ask.

"We're the originals," Princess Vanny says proudly. "We four have entertained hundreds—"

"Thousands," Taffyta corrects.

"Thousands of players. Just us four."

"That *is* impressive," you have to admit.

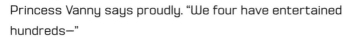

Go to the NEXT PAGE.

The girls get into their karts. When they do, you realize there isn't a kart for you.

Princess Vanny must have guessed how disappointed you are to miss out on this race. She comes up to you and puts a hand on your shoulder. **"Use my car,"** she offers.

"Are you sure?" you ask.

She nods firmly. "One princess to another, this is one race I have to see!"

You hop into her kart and test the engine. At first it coughs and sputters, but in just a few moments you hear that gorgeous familiar hum.

Around you the other drivers are turning on their engines. They also take a bit of time to warm up, but the karts sound like they're in good condition once they get going.

"Ready, set—drive!" Princess Vanny drops the starting flag—and you're off!

The tracks aren't as twisty, and there are fewer obstacles to navigate in this game. The karts aren't as fast, either. But the game is challenging because parts of it are completely different and new, at least to you. Seeing the other racers happy to be driving again is exhilarating, and you make a mental note to thank Ralph for finding the wheel so you could play this version of *Sugar Rush*.

You pull over the finish line just inches ahead of Taffyta. A moment later Minty and Crumbelina barrel through. You give each other high fives.

Go to the *NEXT PAGE*.

"That was fun!" Taffyta exclaims. Her face is glowing.

"We should definitely keep driving, even if no one is playing," Minty says.

"Can we, Princess Vanny?" Crumbelina asks.

"Of course we can!" Princess Vanny says.

"It was great to meet you," you tell them. "But I'd better get going. People waiting, and all that."

You hug each of the girls. Weird to think of it, but Princess Vanny is like your great-great-great-grandmother.

She tugs your arm and leads you away to have a private conversation.

"Can I go with you? To your game?" she asks.

You're so surprised all you can do is blink.

What do you think?

Say yes and take her to your **Sugar Rush** *on PAGE 227.*

Or say no and explain why on PAGE 108.

Now it's your turn to be incredulous. "Whoa. That's a lot of friends. How can you hang out with all of them?"

Yesss laughs. "Silly! We don't hang out. Not **IRL**."

"Huh?"

"In. Real. Life," she explains. She studies you. "I guess you don't text, either."

You shrug. "Don't need to. I'm with my friends all the time. IRL."

Go to the NEXT PAGE.

Her eyes widen behind her snazzy glasses. "Offline friends. Amazing! I haven't met most of my ten million–plus friends."

You shake your head. "I don't know . . . Does that count as having friends?"

"Of course it does!" Yesss stands and snaps her fingers, and another screen appears. This one isn't a movie, though. It's a list. A looooooong list. Next to each name is a little picture of a person. She gestures to the screen. **"Voilà! My friends list."**

"That's a lot of names all right," you say. "But who's your *best* friend? I have friends like Felix Jr. and Zombie and Gene. But Vanellope is special. She's my *best* friend. And I'm hers. And she's who I have to find."

You swallow hard. Just talking about your friends is making you homesick. Are you ever going to find Vanellope? Find the steering wheel? Find your way home?

Go to the NEXT PAGE.

Yesss sits back down. "*Best* friend?" she repeats. She tilts her head, thinking. "Hmm. I have lots of lists of bests," she says. "Best Movies, Best Cooking Hacks, Best Hairstyle, Best Funny Animal Video and *all* of its subcategories. But I've never seen a Best Friend list."

"It's not a list," you protest. "It's a *who*."

"A *who*? What do you mean?" she asks. She looks sincerely interested, so you think hard. You want to explain it just right.

"A best friend is someone who you like hanging out with so much that you could do it all day every day. Forever," you say. "Someone who gets you. Who doesn't mind if you goof up sometimes. Who has the most hilarious laugh that it makes you laugh, too. Who makes even worse jokes than you do. Who gives you ridiculous nicknames. Who loves it when your names for her are even more ridiculous. Who saw the good in you when no one else did. And vice versa." You let out a long sigh. "You know. A *best friend*."

To your surprise, Yesss is silent. This is the first time she hasn't run somewhere or started chattering a mile a minute. Then you see she is discreetly wiping her eyes with a little hankie.

"You okay?" you ask.

"Me? I'm fine. You just got me thinking . . . well . . . never mind."

Go to the NEXT PAGE.

And just like that she's back to her high-energy self. She jumps up, then changes her hairstyle, her outfit, and her lipstick in the blink of an eye. "Okay, you've convinced me. We've got to find your friend."

You stand, too. "I'd really like to find the steering wheel she needs first, if that's okay," you say. "That way I can save the game for her."

Yesss gives you an indulgent smile. "Awww." She waggles a finger at you. "You want to be her hero."

You look down at your feet. "Well, she does kind of think of me that way."

"And we're not going to let her down! Time for some serious multitasking!"

She pats the seat beside her. You sit.

Turn to PAGE 83.

You and Vanellope stand in the middle of a dance floor. You're in the game *Bust a Move*. Multicolored neon lights flash, and thumping music makes the floor vibrate. All around you people are leaping, twirling, stomping, and generally dancing like maniacs.

Vanellope looks up at you and says something.

"What?" you shout. The music is so loud you can't hear her.

She tries again.

You cup your hand behind your ear and bend down closer. "What'd you say?" you shout again.

"I said," she shouts into your ear, "what kind of game is this?"

You straighten back up. "Sheesh," you complain. "You trying to make me deaf?"

She glitches up to your shoulder. "I'm not, but this game might."

The music suddenly stops and a space clears on the dance floor. "We're ready for the first round of *Bust a Move*," an announcer booms. "Dancers, take your places!"

"A dance contest?" you say. "I'm not so sure about—"

Before you can finish your sentence, dancers surround you. You and Vanellope are shoved into the center of the dance floor.

Stumble to PAGE 56.

You and Vanellope leave the *Fix-It Felix, Jr.* game and head to Game Central Station. You hide behind one of the columns. You peer around it.

Uh-oh.

Surge Protector is patrolling the barricaded Wi-Fi plug. There's no way you can get to the Internet with him in the way.

"What do we do now?" Vanellope asks.

Do you trap him? Try that on PAGE 8.

Or do you distract him? That might work on PAGE 170.

YOU ARE YESSS

. . . **YESSS!** Trend-spotting, cutting-edge Yesss. Yes, you are now Yesss. And you need to make a choice about what to do next.

Ralph's devotion to his best friend, Vanellope, makes you want to connect with your old pals on PAGE 157.

Ralph's lack of knowledge about the Internet gets you thinking about a time when you were equally clueless. Hard to believe, but it's true. There was a time when you weren't the glam expert you are now. And since nothing on the Internet is ever truly lost, you can go back to when it all began, before you were the fabulous version of yourself you are now.

Go back to that time on PAGE 175.

Or maybe you should stay on point and focus on searching for the steering wheel on PAGE 218.

You type a quick message to No. It takes only an instant before a return message pops up on your screen. Your heart sinks. No has **blocked** you.

What did you do that made him so angry he'd actually block you?

You tap your glasses to click to his profile.

"Ha!" No hasn't just blocked *you*. Nope. No has blocked *everyone*.

Why am I surprised? you ask yourself.

That's just how No is. Always so negative.

Try reaching Perhaps on PAGE 169.

Ping! Ping! Ping! You grin as the notifications come flying in. Your eyes narrow as you study the results. You drag the false leads to the trash. You reject one after another. You're not worried. There are always far more wrong answers than right ones for a search like this.

The notifications begin to slow down. You continue deleting the ones that aren't very promising. This makes your screen a lot less cluttered and much easier to read.

Bingo!

"I do believe we have a winner," you murmur.

Go to PAGE 140.

You sneak a peek from the edge of the screen. Mr. Litwak is coming out of his office. He has a big smile on his face.

"Good news, kids!" he announces. "I just got an e-mail from eBay! A *Sugar Rush* steering wheel is on its way!"

The kids cheer.

You beam.

"We did it!"

"We sure did," Ralph says.

"Is that Vanellope in *Fix-It Felix, Jr.*?" you hear a kid ask. He points at the screen.

OOOOPS!

You drop down flat. Though it's hard to stay out of sight when you're cracking up laughing. You feel so good, you're giddy.

Yep, it all worked out in . . .

THE END.

"**Fun!**" Vanellope squeals. She jumps down from your shoulder and charges for the socket.

"Stop!" Surge Protector steps in front of the socket. Vanellope skids to a stop.

"The Internet is nothing to laugh at." Surge Protector crosses his arms and blocks everyone's view of the new plug-in. "It is new and it is different, therefore we should fear it. So keep out. And get to work. The arcade's about to open."

Head for your games on the NEXT PAGE.

"Figures," Vanellope says. She peers over her shoulder toward the Wi-Fi socket as you walk away together. "We finally get something new plugged in and we're not even allowed to go in there."

"Yeah," you agree, "Surge Protector would hate to see us have a good time."

"A new racing game would have been cool," she sighs.

"Why?" You're surprised by how wistful she sounds. "Something wrong with your game?"

"No. It's just—" She turns back around and shrugs. "Every bonus level's been unlocked. I know every shortcut. I'd love a new track."

"New track?" you ask.

"Yeah," Vanellope says. "Don't you ever wish something new and different would happen in your game?"

"No," you say honestly.

Vanellope shakes her head. "Well, agree to disagree."

"Wait," you say, "you disagree? You don't think life is perfect?"

"No, it's just something you say to end an argument," Vanellope says.

"We're arguing?" you ask, alarmed. "I don't wanna argue."

"Relax, relax," Vanellope says, trying to calm you down. "You're making it worse. Go to work. I'll see you tonight, Dung Merchant."

You nod. "All right."

As you walk away, something occurs to you.

Turn to PAGE 5.

You hate to disappoint her, but you know what you have to say.

"I'm so sorry," you tell Princess Vanny. "I wish I could, but your game needs you. Every *Sugar Rush* needs its Vanellope."

"I suppose you're right," she says.

"Keep racing!" you tell her as you rejoin the girls. "And we'll stay in touch. There's this thing called e-mail I heard about."

You sneak out of the game, taking care to avoid the guard in the vintage arcade game museum.

You quickly find your way back to KnowsMore's kiosk, where Ralph is waiting for you. He gives you the good news: your replacement steering wheel is already on its way to Litwak's Family Fun Center!

"Have fun?" he asks you as you head back to Game Central Station.

"I did," you say. "But you know what, Ralph? There really is no place like home."

THE END.

You slowly make your way down the hall. Each archway provides a glimpse of intriguing places to explore. You plan to check out each and every possibility!

You continue on as your attention is pulled in a million-bajillion different directions. There are characters roaming around, and you decide that you want to see every corner of this place, from the quizzes and trailers to the games and articles. The question is whether or not you'll have time.

After what feels like hours of exploring, you're tired and sweaty from your adventure, so you take a quick break to scan the list of activities you picked up at a kiosk. "I believe I'll go watch a video next," you say.

Turn to PAGE 122.

"What is *with* you?" you demand. "Why can't we get near you?"

"I'm a **Surge Protector**," he snaps. "I'm not made of the same stuff as you and her." Vanellope glitches in frustration. He frowns. "Well, maybe a bit like her."

You help Vanellope to her feet. "One more time?" you ask her.

She has a determined expression on her face. "Can't give up now!"

Once again, you throw yourselves at Surge. And once again you get an electric shock. Only this time, everything in Game Central Station shuts down at once.

Go to the *NEXT PAGE.*

You sit in total darkness. "What happened?" you ask.

"Exactly what I was afraid might happen," Surge says, fuming. "There was a **power surge**. And I wasn't in position to protect it. So the circuits overloaded and *wham*!" He gestures widely. "This is the result."

You gaze around, your eyes slowly adjusting to the darkness. Not a single light is on. Not a single beeper beeps. No electronically generated music plays.

"Um . . ." you hear Vanellope begin tentatively, "sorry?"

"Yeah. Sorry," you say to Surge. "So . . . now what?"

Turn to PAGE 91.

Once you and Ralph can hear each other, you say, "We should probably get back to our plan."

"Plan? Oh, right! Our plan! Mission: Steering Wheel."

"But where do you think it could be?" You turn in a slow circle. "There's a whole lot of Internet out there."

"Maybe we should ask someone," Ralph suggests.

You scan the area. You notice something surprising. "Looks like there are two kinds of folks here," you observe. "Some who resemble us, and those really small square-heads." You point to a flat fellow who looks like he was cut out of cardboard.

A broad-shouldered man wearing a uniform and a badge steps up to you and Ralph. "Do you need to relay something to that avatar?"

"Excuse you?" you ask.

Go to the **NEXT PAGE.**

"You were pointing at that avatar." He keeps his thumbs tucked into his belt and tips his head toward the flat square-headed fellow.

His eyes flick from you to Ralph and back to you again. He must notice your blank expressions, because he continues his explanation. "Avatars. They represent the humans visiting the Internet."

"Ahhhhh," you say, light dawning. You turn to Ralph. "It's just like in the arcade! Humans out there"—you open your arms wide—"affect what goes on in here!"

"Ahhhh," says Ralph.

"That's why we saw that little Litwak," you realize. "The real Mr. Litwak was going onto the Internet."

"Ahhhh," Ralph says again.

"The ones who look like us are, well, like us! They live here."

"Ahhhhhhhhh."

"First-time visitors?" the security guard asks. Then he studies you more closely. "Or are you some kind of malware? Have you been through quarantine? Been checked for viruses?"

What is this guy talking about?

Go to the *NEXT PAGE.*

"Are you implying there might be something wrong with us?" Ralph asks. He looks insulted and takes a menacing step forward.

You grab Ralph's arm. "We're fit as a fiddle," you tell the security guard. "Which is a kind of weird saying. I mean, how unfit could a violin be? Well, I guess if it didn't have any strings, or . . ."

"We're here to find a replacement part for this one's arcade game," Ralph says, jerking his thumb toward you.

"Ah. Shoppers." The security guard nods. "You'll find a lot of shoppers here. Just be careful. Where there are shoppers there are scam artists. **Spammers.** Misleading pop-ups."

"Oh, we know how to take care of ourselves," you assure the security guard.

"Yeah, we're not a pair of numbskulls," Ralph says. "No matter what Surge says."

Turn to **PAGE 70**.

"Okay, here we go," you say. You drop a huge pile of supplies in front of Vanellope. She has joined you in your game, *Fix-It Felix, Jr.* The two of you are on the roof of the building you wreck. After a lackluster performance today, Felix barely needed to fix it.

"I raided Gene's fridge. Good news, he has pie. Oh, and I took a bunch of his pillows and junk." You start arranging them. "I'm thinking we make a fort up here. Or yurt. Or we could stack the pillows and make an igloo. A pillow igloo. A **pigloo**!"

Usually, Vanellope would come back with some wordplay of her own. Or at least laugh. "So whaddya think, kid?" you prompt. "Fort, yurt, or the obvious best choice, pigloo?"

Vanellope lets out a long sigh. "I can't believe I don't have a game anymore. What am I gonna do all day?"

Oh, no. Get her off this topic on the
NEXT PAGE.

    You need to cheer her up. Help her see how cool this is going to be.

    "Are you kidding?" you ask. "That's the best part. You sleep in. You do no work. Then you hang out with me every night!" You sigh contentedly. "I've literally just described paradise!"

Go to the **NEXT PAGE.**

"But I *loved* my game," she protests.

"Oh, come on." You gape at her. "You were just bellyaching about it being too easy!"

"That doesn't mean I didn't love it." She sits and hugs her knees to her chest. "Yeah, sure, it was predictable, but still, I never *really* knew what might happen in a race."

Vanellope's voice grows wistful. "And it's that feeling—the not-knowing-what's-coming-next feeling—that's the stuff. That feels like life to me." She turns to you, her eyes big and shiny with tears. "And if I'm not a racer anymore . . . who am I?"

"You're my **best friend**," you say.

"That's not enough," she replies.

You feel like she kicked you in the gut. "Hey," you say.

She sighs. "No, I just . . ."

She glitches involuntarily, which makes you worry.

"Are you—are you okay?" you ask.

She shakes it off, stopping the glitch. "It's fine," she says. "I'm fine. It's nothing."

She pauses, shaking her head. "I'm sorry, I know I'm being weird. I think maybe I just need to be alone right now."

Turn to **PAGE 25.**

You step out carefully, on the lookout for jungle creatures and biting insects.

Hmm. This doesn't look like a jungle. No trees. No rivers. And it doesn't look as though there are any snakes or crocodiles.

Instead, as far as you can see is a forest of shelves, containers, boxes, and bins.

"This place *is* amazing," you murmur.

"No," a netizen pushing a shopping cart responds. "This is Amazon."

"I thought the Amazon was a jungle with a river and animals and stuff," you say.

"You could probably find some of that stuff for sale here," the netizen says. "Check sporting goods. Or maybe DVDs. Or books. There are a lot of categories."

You look around in wonder at miles of shelves stacked with items. "Who's that?" you ask the netizen. "It looks like a person. Sort of."

"That? That's an avatar."

Go to the NEXT PAGE.

"**A what-now?**" You study the avatar. It's a woman with her hair in rollers, wearing a housedress.

"Someone out in the world is shopping," the netizen explains. "She's scrolling through a page of chairs. Her avatar is her representative here in Amazon. See?"

Oh, right. That mail delivery person explained it to you. That little Litwak you and Vanellope saw before you arrived in the Internet must have been Litwak's avatar! "Got it," you say.

You watch as the avatar studies a gigantic screen rolling through chair options. When a rocking chair appears on the screen, she presses a button. Suddenly, the exact chair appears in the netizen's cart.

"**A sale!**" the netizen exclaims. "Let's get this baby through checkout!" She pushes the shopping cart along one of the aisles. You follow, curious to see what will happen.

The netizen pulls up to a long conveyor belt. The avatar stands on the opposite side. She pulls out a wallet. Suddenly, she freezes. Her face goes blank.

"Is she all right?" you ask the netizen.

You jump over the conveyer belt and walk up to the avatar. "You okay, miss?" You wave your hand in front of her face. "He-llloooo? Anyone in there?"

Go to the NEXT PAGE.

"Don't bother," the netizen tells you. "She's gone. The sale didn't go through."

"What happened?" you ask.

"The human clicked on another website." The netizen sighs. "It happens all the time. Now I've got to return this chair. It seems like I spend my days taking things off shelves and then putting them back on." She sounds frustrated.

"Why wouldn't she just get the chair?" you ask. "She looked at all those others. She picked it out. . . ."

The netizen shrugs. "She got distracted. It's easy online. There's always another website to visit. Another special offer or deal of the day."

"What could distract . . . Hey, what's that?"

Go to the NEXT PAGE.

Flashing neon arrows catch your eye. They're all pointing to a side door. The sign above the door reads **THIS WAY TO INSTAGRAM!**

You step through the door and gasp. You're standing in what seems to be a ginormous museum.

"Look at all the pictures!" You turn in a slow circle, trying to take it all in. The pictures seem to go on forever.

What kind of place is this? In one corner, pictures are flipping, as if a giant were riffling through them. Off to the side, pictures appear and then disappear. With all the movement, you're pretty sure Instagram isn't a museum. "It must be a game."

Oooh. Maybe if you win this game, you'll get another medal. You do love your medals. Or you could win a present for Vanellope.

Maybe if you give Vanellope a present, she will forgive you for what happened to *Sugar Rush*. You had only good intentions. But it still wound up causing trouble.

Never mind. You're in the Internet now. You'll find the replacement wheel and everything will be set right. But first there's this Instagram place to investigate!

"Hmmmm. So how does this game work?" You rub your hands together. "Only one way to find out."

Play Instagram on **PAGE 77.**

OhMyDisney keeps you so entertained you lose track of time. You're watching action-packed movie trailers when an e-mail delivery truck arrives with a message for you. You hit pause and take the note. "'I found the steering wheel!'" you read. "'Love, Ralph.'"

You grin. *Sugar Rush* has been saved!

And hanging out in this cool place is totally worth having to wash Ralph's stinky drawers for a week.

There's so much to do here, you may take your time before heading home. And you're definitely bringing Ralph next time.

After all, adventures are best when they're shared.

THE END.

You're closing in on the target.

"Oh, no!" you wail. An avatar is stepping up to the booth. "Ralph! What if that guy in the Hawaiian shirt gets the steering wheel first?"

"Ain't gonna happen, li'l sis. Not on my watch." He thunders through the crowd. Avatars yelp and fling themselves out of the way. Including Mr. Hawaiian Shirt.

"That steering wheel is ours!" Ralph bellows.

The clerk cowers behind the counter. "Not a problem."

Ralph peers down at Mr. Hawaiian Shirt, who's struggling to get back to his sandaled feet. "How about you? You got a problem with that?"

You make a fist and wave it at the guy. "Do ya?"

Does he? Find out on **PAGE 265.**

You don't want to miss the start of the race, so you wheel the bike to the starting line. "Excuse me, pardon me," you say as you make your way from the shed into the road.

"Winners coming through," Vanellope pipes up.

You find a spot near the center of the line of professional riders.

"Nice outfit," you tell the guy next to you. He's wearing a skintight bright cobalt-blue shirt and tights. Logos cover his torso.

He eyes you up and down. "You too," he says in a thick French accent. "I like your mascot," he says, nodding toward Vanellope.

"I'm no mascot," she informs him. "I'm your biggest nightmare."

He looks confused, then goes back to concentrating on the road ahead of him.

"Okay," you tell Vanellope. "Let me get my balance, then you glitch up to the handlebars. We'll give 'em something to watch."

"Okie-doke!"

You swing your leg over the seat and hop up. You place your feet on the pedals.

The bike wobbles. Before Vanellope can move, the bike shatters beneath you. You lose your balance and topple over onto the racer next to you.

Like dominoes, the entire line of riders falls over.

Ooops!

You gave 'em something to watch all right. But no one expected it to be this!

Head back to PAGE 167 to try a different wheel.

You hurry back inside your game. Camping out on top of the building was a fun idea, but it isn't *your* place. It's where all the **Nicelanders** live. And while they're nice and all, Vanellope barely knows most of them. She might not feel comfortable there when she's feeling sad. Like she is today.

Your place is the dump. A place she's been a gazillion times. Her home away from home. You figure that's where she may go after she finishes being alone.

And there she is, sitting on a pile of bricks.

Go to the NEXT PAGE.

You dash over to her, dislodging a few bricks along the way. "If they shut down *Sugar Rush*, we'll find you a new game," you say in a big burst. "One you like just as much."

She glances up at you, dubious. She frowns, then says, "But it's not just about me. What about everyone else in *Sugar Rush*?"

You've thought of that, too. "We'll find games for all of the other drivers, too! But you get first dibs, 'cause you're friends with the big cheese." You stick your thumb under the strap of your overalls and puff out your chest.

"Yeah, you are pretty cheesy." She gives you a weak smile.

You can see you haven't totally convinced her. But at least she's trying.

Turn to PAGE 132.

You land in a bramble of raspberry hard candies. The drivers reverse again and head back the way they came.

Phew. That was close.

What's the next one? You try to remember the signs you and Felix painted.

Oh, right! The obstacle course. But instead of *driving* through it, the drivers have to get out of their karts and *run* through it.

You sneak past the obstacle course, where you hear karts suddenly braking. You also hear a lot of laughter. That's a good sign. You hurry along the track to plant yourself at the finish line.

You chuckle. For the final new challenge, each driver has to stop the kart, stand up in the driver's seat, and sing a song.

Go to the NEXT PAGE.

The finish line is up ahead. The drivers have beaten you there. But you can hear them: Three drivers singing at once. Now four! Now five! And none of them are singing the same song. It's deafening—and hilarious.

Then cheers go up as someone crosses the finish line. Sour Bill makes the announcement over the loudspeakers.

"And it's Taffyta, by point zero, zero, zero, zero one second!"

He sounds shocked. Which is exactly how you feel.

Not to mention worried.

Will Vanellope be upset that she didn't win? She *always* wins this game.

Turn to PAGE 258.

You and Felix post flyers all over Game Central Station announcing the **auditions**. Luckily, the arcade is closed tomorrow, so you can find your replacement Ralph and be set up for the next time Litwak opens for business.

"Remember, this wouldn't be a permanent position," you explain to the characters who show up to try out. "This would be just while Ralph is away."

You and Felix sit at a long table set up in front of the building Ralph wrecks in your game.

"Good turnout," you comment. Some of the arcade's worst Bad Guys and even some big, strong Good Guys have shown up.

"This is going to be fun!" Felix says.

"We'll be done in no time," you say.

Turn to PAGE 248.

A few minutes later, you and all the drivers of *Sugar Rush* peer anxiously through the screen of the game into the arcade. Mr. Litwak stands holding the console's steering wheel. A young girl frowns beside him.

"Mr. Litwak, the Vanellope racer wasn't working, and I think maybe I turned the wheel too hard," the girl says. "I'm real sorry."

"Oh, it's okay, Swati," Mr. Litwak says, studying the console. "I think I can get it back on there pretty easy." He steps forward and places the wheel in position.

You can feel the game shaking as Mr. Litwak fiddles with the wheel, trying to get it to reattach.

Just then, you all hear a loud *SNAP!*

You cringe. Mr. Litwak takes a step back.

Everyone gasps. Your stomach sinks to somewhere around your ankles.

Go to the NEXT PAGE.

Mr. Litwak holds up **two pieces** of steering wheel. It broke when he tried to put it back on!

"Um. Okay," you say, trying to reassure everyone, including yourself. "Still not a problem. Obviously he'll just order a new part."

Mr. Litwak gazes down at the two pieces of the steering wheel. "Well, I'd order a new part, but the company that made *Sugar Rush* went out of business years ago."

What now?

Turn to **PAGE 19**.

"Let's see . . . what would be a good game for you?" You rub your chin, thinking.

"Are there any other racing games?" she asks tentatively. It's as if she's afraid to even hope. It breaks your heart.

You rack your brain. "You know, there was a new game brought in not that long ago. I think it's a race."

You can't remember its name, but you remember where it was plugged in. It's clear on the other side of Game Central Station.

"Should we go check it out?" you say. "No time like the present."

She shrugs. "It's not like I've got anything better to do."

Not exactly the excitement you were hoping for, but it's a start.

But when you and Vanellope arrive at the entrance to the game, she snorts.

"Are you kidding?" She stares up at you, half quizzical, half annoyed.

Go to the NEXT PAGE.

"What?" You point to the name of the game. "*Baby Bonanza* sounds fun."

"Sounds stupid," she complains. "And childish."

You raise an eyebrow. "Hate to tell you, kid, but you *are* a child."

She crosses her arms and glares at you. "I'm a daredevil speed demon. And a princess. Not to mention *president*."

"Sure, but . . . Well, a bonanza is a good thing, right? C'mon, just give it a try."

"I just don't think it's me."

"You won't know until you check it out," you argue. Sheesh. Usually she's up for any adventure!

She sighs. "I'll try it." She doesn't sound very enthusiastic. Then she narrows her eyes and waggles a finger at you. "But only if you play, too."

"Deal."

You enter the game together. When you stand up, you bang your head on the ceiling. Pretty clouds, rainbows, and suns smile down on you. This game was definitely not built for someone your size.

"So, what's the goal of the game?" Vanellope asks.

You slouch to avoid banging your head again and glance around. Plump little babies crawl around cribs, high chairs, and toys. "Looks like they're all racing to get to that pacifier in the middle there."

Vanellope steps over the lane dividers and picks up the pacifier sitting in the bouncy chair. "You mean this one?"

Go to the NEXT PAGE.

"That's not fair, Vanellope," you say. "You're supposed to crawl. And stay *in* the lanes, not step over the dividers."

"Fine." She tosses the pacifier back into the bouncy chair. She stands there, waiting.

"What?"

"Hands and knees, dude. If I have to crawl, you have to crawl."

Sigh. There's no arguing with her when she gets this way.

Crawl to PAGE 26.

Everyone in Game Central Station does their best to keep you and the other *Sugar Rush* drivers distracted. The Nicelanders let you and the drivers work off your frustration by smashing the building. Felix fixes it all up— then you smash it all over again. Calhoun offers to lead a boot camp, but none of the drivers takes her up on it. Doing push-ups and sit-ups doesn't seem very appealing under the circumstances. Taffyta and Crumbelina visit each of the games that include animals. Playing with the cute little critters takes their minds off things. Unfortunately, nothing keeps you from growing ever more anxious.

It's nearly impossible to fall asleep. You toss and turn on the bricks all night. Finally, finally, the sun begins to rise.

Ralph is still asleep. But you can't wait for him. You have to see if Litwak is going to plug your game back in.

Leaving Ralph to wake up, you sprint to the *Fix-It Felix, Jr.* screen. You should be able to see Litwak's Family Fun Center from there.

Yup. Litwak is just arriving to open up for the day. Is he going to plug *Sugar Rush* back in? You hold your breath as he makes his way along the rows of games.

Your heart sinks. He passes *Sugar Rush*, but he doesn't remove the OUT OF ORDER sign.

It didn't work.

Go to the NEXT PAGE.

Ralph lumbers up beside you and sits. He lets out a huge yawn, then says, "What's wrong, little sister?"

"We didn't change anything," you say sadly. "*Sugar Rush* is still destined for the junk heap."

"Too soon to tell," Ralph says. "The Internet moves fast, but I suspect getting that steering wheel into Litwak's hands won't be quite so speedy."

That gives you a new worry. "What if he gets rid of my game before the steering wheel arrives?"

"Now that would be a pickle," Ralph admits.

You press your face against the screen. You can't see Litwak anymore, but you notice a few kids are approaching.

"Time to get to work, I suppose," Ralph says. He looks at you sympathetically. "You want to hang out at the dump today? Or go to Game Central Station? The other racers might be there."

You know you're going to have to do something while your game is unplugged. But all you really want to do is keep watch. Wait and see what Litwak's going to do.

A kid approaches the *Fix-It Felix, Jr.* game. You quickly duck out of sight. You're about to crawl away when you hear a girl ask, "Mr. Litwak, is *Sugar Rush* still unplugged?"

You have to wait to hear what Mr. Litwak says.

Find out on **PAGE 105.**

"Three!"

The music blares again. Up on the screen, Rockin' Roger is doing a simple side-to-side step. Easy!

"Left, right, left, right," you mutter as you try to match Rockin' Roger's every step. So far, so good.

Uh-oh. The moves are getting more complicated. He spins. You spin.

And spin. And spin. And spin. Oh, no! You can't stop!

"Amazing pirouettes!" you hear someone say.

"He's doing the Wrecking Ball!" someone else exclaims.

You hold your arms out for balance. You teeter and totter. Vanellope isn't helping. She's still on your shoulder, but her arms are wrapped around your face. You can't see!

Your legs criss and cross as you desperately try to stay upright.

"Look what he's doing now!"

"We should try it!"

You rotate your arms like a windmill as you try to stay standing. But it's no use! You lose your balance and land on your backside. Vanellope tumbles off your shoulder and onto your lap.

Go to the NEXT PAGE.

You shake your head, dazed, and look around. "Huh?"

All across the dance floor, the contestants are windmilling their arms! In unison, they all drop to the floor.

The screens display Rockin' Roger standing still, just staring out at you.

"We have a new winner!" the announcer declares.

An elegant man in a tuxedo rushes up to you and Vanellope.

He grabs your hand. You think he's going to help you up, but he just pumps it up and down. Vanellope hops off your lap. "Congratulations," the man gushes. "You are the new champion!"

"I am?" You slowly get to your feet.

"You were so good the dancers stopped paying any attention to Rockin' Roger. They just wanted to follow *you!*"

"They did?" you and Vanellope say in unison. She's as shocked as you are.

"We would like to offer you the lead dancer spot," the man continues.

Wow. You never in a million years would have dreamed that you could become the star of a brand-new game. Rockin' Ralph!

"Only if Vanellope here is my permanent partner," you say.

"Ohhhh, no," Vanellope says, backing away. "I'd need hazard pay! Dancing with you is far more dangerous than anything I'm up against in *Sugar Rush!*"

Oh, well. Time to choose a different game on PAGE 189.

Then words start appearing. *On the one hand,* you read, *it would be wonderful to catch up with you. On the other, we barely know each other anymore. Perhaps it will be awkward.*

How do I respond to that? you wonder.

Before you can, though, she sends more messages. *On the one hand, maybe it would be a good way to truly patch things up. Perhaps—*

We're meeting, you type back, interrupting her message. *Name where and when.*

I don't know, she replies. *We could meet in an hour. Or perhaps it would be better to meet tomorrow? Or next week?*

Now you remember why you and Perhaps had a falling-out. But who can't use more friends? Perhaps it's time to get over your differences. You're good at making decisions, Perhaps is good at considering all of the information. There might be a way that you can play to both of your strengths.

Tomorrow, you reply. *I'll pick you up.*

You feel good about reconnecting with Perhaps. After all, the best of friends can always find common ground in . . .

THE END.

Before you click on the image of the steering wheel, you'd better check in with the big guy. You want to be sure you found the one he's looking for before ordering it from eBay for him.

The big lug is snoring loudly. You reach out and tap him gently on the shoulder.

"**Whatzzat?**" he shouts as he sits bolt upright. His head whips around.

You leap back. "Chill, dude," you say. "I think I have a line on that steering wheel."

"Wheel?" He rubs his face and yawns. "Oh, right." He looks around again, more slowly. "I'm in the Internet. Looking for a *Sugar Rush* steering wheel." He slumps. "And I can't find Vanellope."

Go to the NEXT PAGE.

"Buck up, big guy." You punch his shoulder lightly. "It's all under control. Didn't I tell you? I've got **connections.**"

"And a list of ten million friends you've never met," Ralph says sleepily. "Did one of them find it?"

"Actually, no! I put a watch on a site that lets me keep track of—never mind," you say as you see confusion replace sleepiness in Ralph's eyes. "Now all I need is for you to make sure the wheel I found is the one you're looking for. It can be delivered wherever you want in a nanosecond. I'll call in a favor from one of those friends and it will all be taken care of just like that." You snap your fingers. "Faster, even."

He brightens. "That's great! Thanks!"

Turn to **PAGE 291**.

"Oh, no you don't," Surge Protector says, quickly blocking your path.

"But—"

Surge Protector crosses his arms and glares at you. He takes a step toward you. You can tell he means business. But you can't just leave Vanellope in the Internet. She may be in trouble!

You catch Felix's eye. You tip your head toward the socket.

Felix points at himself and mouths, *Me?*

You nod furiously, then shake your head toward the socket again. He looks confused.

"Are you all right?" Surge Protector asks. "Are you glitching?"

"I, um, I'm just thinking how great it would be if *someone* could go into that socket and bring Vanellope back out." You make your eyes super big and glare at Felix.

"Ohhhhhh," Felix says, finally understanding. He leaps into the socket behind Surge Protector.

Finally. You thought he'd never get your signal!

Turn to *PAGE 159*.

"We better get back," Vanellope says. "We don't want Surge Protector to notice we're gone."

Ralph nods, and they turn to go, but Ralph turns back. "Don't be a stranger," he tells you.

"Wouldn't dream of it," you promise. "After all, I'm on your top ten list!"

As you watch the two friends disappear back into the socket, you sigh.

Ralph wasn't exactly a trendsetter. Or a tech-savvy dude. Or even knowledgeable about, well, much. But you definitely learned something from him. You learned what it means to be a best friend—or at least a top ten friend.

"You know," you muse as you head toward the Search Bar, "I think I'm going to start spending more time with my friends in real life. And I'm going to start by looking up a few right now."

THE END
(and a beginning!)

Surge Protector rushes over. "Did you go into the Wi-Fi?" he demands. "Were you in the Internet?"

"Um . . . well . . ."

"I told you it was dangerous in there!" Surge scolds. "There's a **reason** I blocked it off!"

A group of game characters swarms you. "What was it like? Did you really go into the Internet?"

You scan over the heads of the people clamoring with questions. "Where's Vanellope?" you ask.

"We haven't seen her," Gene, one of the Nicelanders, tells you.

You whirl around and stare at the socket you just emerged from. "Oh, no! She's still inside!"

Turn to PAGE 142.

Ralph is a lot calmer now that you're down on the ground. In fact, he seems entranced by a flock of blue birds tweeting nearby.

He follows them. You follow *him*. Pretty soon, you stand beside him at the edge of a pretty park.

"Hey, Ralph, why is the grass blue?" you ask.

Then you realize it's not grass. The park is so filled with little blue birds that not one blade is visible.

"What *is* this place?" you say. The birds are making such a racket you have to yell to be heard. "Why are all the birds congregating here?"

"It's a **Twitter** feed," a passerby tells you. He glances up at the sky. Millions of blue birds are flying toward the park. "Someone must have tweeted something particularly interesting. Now it's trending like crazy. Hashtag 'popular,' I'd say."

"Huh?" Ralph says.

But the guy has moved on.

You start to enter the park, but Ralph stops you. "You know . . . maybe that's not the best idea."

You frown. "Why not?"

Find out on **PAGE 288**.

Very soon you and Vanellope are being rowed out to an island. The sailors drop you off and quickly return to the schooner.

"Hello!" A netizen floats above you. "Where'd you come from?"

"We got thrown off that boat," Vanellope declares. She sounds kinda proud.

"We need to get back to Game Central Station," you explain. "How will we do that?"

"There should be another boat coming along soon," the boy says.

"What is this place?" Vanellope asks, looking around at the island, which seems to have portals—not unlike plugs—that lead to more places.

"This is where we can play games. Want to be on my team?"

You and Vanellope look at each other, then simultaneously shout, **"YES!"**

THE END.

You race after the pod. It pauses on what looks like a loading platform. That gives you just enough time to catch up to it—moments before it's launched into a tube.

You hear Ralph's thudding footsteps behind you. "I bet this place is the Internet version of Game Central Station," you tell him breathlessly when he catches up to you. "And the real Internet is in there!"

The minute you point at the tube, you're encased in a pod—just like the mini Litwak. The pod lurches forward.

"Woo-hoo!" You're moving so fast everything outside the pod is just a blur. You hear Ralph bellowing behind you.

"You okay back there?" you call.

"No! This thing is **too tight**! I can't breathe!"

"Hang in there, buddy!"

He may not be having the comfiest ride, but at least he's with you.

You can't wait to find out where you're going to land!

Go to PAGE 184.

Vanellope zooms straight at you. She comes to a stop mere inches from your toes, brakes squealing. She jumps out and glitches to the hood of her kart. **"Well done, citizens of *Sugar Rush*!"** she declares.

The other drivers pull up, surrounding you.
Gulp.

What are they going to do?
Find out on the NEXT PAGE.

"We really showed them what we're made of!" Vanellope tells the other drivers. "And I have to say, it was the best. Game. *Ever!*"

All the drivers cheer.

Your mouth falls open. "You—you liked it?" you stammer.

"You bet we liked it!" Vanellope replies. "Didn't we?"

The drivers cheer again. They all start chattering at once, comparing stunts, tricks, and highlights.

Vanellope sidles up closer to you. "I have a feeling you were the one responsible for the miraculous mayhem."

You study the drivers. They do look energized. More excited than you've seen them in a while.

"Well, you *did* say you wanted a challenge," you tell Vanellope.

She claps her hands for attention. "Today, instead of racing each other, we worked as a team!" she declares. "Everyone took part. As your president-princess, I declare us *all* winners." She grasps your hand and holds it up as if you're a champion. "Including you, Ralph. For coming up with this spectacular idea."

"Awww, shucks," you say.

Vanellope beams up at you. "I can't wait to see what you and your crew are going to do tomorrow!"

Your plan was an A-number-one hit. It succeeded beyond your wildest dreams.

Now all you have to do is convince the terrified Bad Guys to do it all again!

THE END.

Once again, you and Ralph are each encased in a pod and launched into a tube. In the blink of an eye, you're deposited in a gigantic warehouse.

Rows and rows of booths create crooked aisles. Avatars scramble to beat each other to stalls. Everyone seems to be shouting at once.

"Going once, going twice, sold!" someone shouts. "To CatLover73 in Omaha!"

"Who would like to bid on this genuine imitation leather replica of—"

"I've got fifty, do I hear fifty-five?"

"The clock is ticking, ladies and gentleman, get your bids in—"

You cover your ears. It's deafening!

Then you feel Ralph tugging your hands away. "What?" you demand.

"I said, I think I found it!"

"You did?" You glitch up to his shoulder so you can see above the bustling crowd. "Where?"

He points his thick finger straight ahead.

"**'Vintage Arcade Games,'**" you read with reverence. "Well, my trusty steed, whatcha waitin' for?"

Ralph gallops you to **PAGE 3**.

"I can get you there," KnowsMore says. "But it will be up to the proprietor whether or not you can have a 'test run.'"

"Sure, sure, sure." Your eyes dart among the five pictures of *Sugar Rush*. You have no doubt you'll be able to talk your way into playing at least one game.

You point at the earliest version of the game. "That one," you declare.

KnowsMore hits a key and *whoosh*! A pod wraps itself around you and off you go!

Arrive on the NEXT PAGE.

A short ride later, you come to a stop. The pod vanishes and you find yourself in a vast, brightly lit space. Large picture windows line long walls. Inside each one is an arcade game. In each wall are archways leading to more rooms with displays. A placard on the wall reads VINTAGE GAMES. FIRST EDITIONS. Signs over the archways list what the other rooms hold: PINBALL MACHINES, SECOND EDITIONS, NEW-AND-IMPROVED.

"Whoa," you say, your eyes growing big. "It's like a museum just for arcade games."

You stroll along the displays of the first editions. "Ha! Is that what Gonzo originally looked like?" You pass another familiar game. "Why, look at that. *Fix-It Felix, Jr.* hasn't changed since the very first console."

You stop in front of a display that has a DISCONTINUED sign hanging from it. "'*Booger Bombs*'?" you read. You shake your head. "Whose bright idea was that game?" You're not surprised it didn't catch on.

Time's a'wasting. Find the first Sugar Rush on the NEXT PAGE.

You find the earlier version of *Sugar Rush*. There you are on the screen! You wave at yourself. Your other self doesn't wave back. That's when you realize you're not looking at the real game. It's a picture of one in a catalog.

"Please don't touch the merchandise," someone says in a bored voice.

You turn and see a woman with a clipboard approaching you. Eyeglasses dangle from a chain around her neck. A mass of curls is piled on her head.

"Purchase order," she says, staring at her clipboard.

"I don't have one," you say.

She tears something off her clipboard and holds it out to you without even raising her eyes. "Come back after you fill this out in triplicate."

You don't take the paper. "But I don't have that kind of time," you say.

She glances at you. Then she lowers her clipboard and takes a longer look. "You look familiar."

You brighten. "That's me!" You point to the screen of the original *Sugar Rush*. You dash to it and stand in front of it. You point at yourself, then you point at the picture.

"What are you doing out of your game?" she demands.

"No—I—" Then you stop yourself.

You have a feeling you just found your way in.

Get into the game on PAGE 226.

Get into the game on PAGE 226.

You and Vanellope follow Calhoun to a locker room. "First thing we need to do is get you **outfitted**." She reaches into a locker and starts tossing gear at you.

You leap around, trying to catch all the items flying through the air. You hear Vanellope let out a few yelps.

Calhoun turns. "What is going on? And where's the recruit?"

You look around. You're holding one of the canisters used to fight the cy-bugs. There's a pile on the floor in front of you: uniform, walkietalkie, boots, and other equipment. "Vanellope?"

"Under here," she says from under the pile.

Go to the **NEXT PAGE**.

"Quit fooling around," Calhoun snaps. "When the go signal comes, you've got to be ready in an instant. You hear me? In. An. Instant!" she bellows into the pile covering Vanellope.

"Yeah, yeah, yeah," Vanellope mutters as she emerges from the heap.

You help her get into the uniform. Only it's waaaaaaay too big for her. The sleeves dangle to the ground, and she trips over the pant legs with every step she takes. Still, Vanellope is willing to try.

You follow her to the loading dock. She's tiny next to the other soldiers. You start to get nervous. Is she going to be okay?

The alarm sounds and everyone starts running.
Even you.

Race to *PAGE 68.*

"It's too easy to get lost in this place," you tell Vanellope. "We should stick together."

"Good plan, my man," Vanellope says. She glitches down from your shoulder. The battling search engines crowd around you again.

"Back off!" you bellow. The search engines cower a moment, then begin to approach again.

You raise your fist. "We're going with the little guy," you tell them. "Because he's the only one who has been polite."

"But—" the search engine with the headset starts. You glare at him and he stops. They all slink away.

"Thank you," KnowsMore says. "You have come to the right place." His hands hover over a keyboard.

"We're looking for a wheel—" you begin.

Before you can finish your sentence, images appear on the counter in front of you.

"Wow. That's a lot of wheels." You scratch your head. "A lot of places to search."

Turn to PAGE 167.

You tiptoe away from the snoring Ralph. You pull up your enormous friends list again.

You know exactly whom you're looking for. You're going to do something outrageous and ask them to meet you IRL. It's been a long time, but you hope they'll agree. They were your friends, back when friends existed *only* in real life.

You scan your friends list, searching for your old pals **Perhaps** and **No**.

There they are!

Just one question.
Who do you contact first,
No or Perhaps?

Send a message to No on PAGE 103.

Send a message to Perhaps on PAGE 169.

"How about one of your top ten?" you suggest. "Those lists always go over well."

"Sure," Ralph agrees. He counts on his fingers. "There's Vanellope, of course. And Felix. And his wife, Calhoun. I guess we're friends. Oh, and Sour Bill. And Zombie."

"Sounds as if you run in some very interesting circles, my friend," you tell him.

"I think if we count all the Nicelanders as one friend," he continues, "then there should be room for you in a list of ten."

You're surprised how pleased you are. In fact, you're pretty sure you're blushing.

"If we're friends, you really need to meet Vanellope," Ralph says.

"Of course. But first things first." You gesture to the screen. "Is that the elusive wheel?"

"Yes!"

"Yes, it is? Or were you just saying my name?"

He picks you up in a crushing bear hug. "Yes, it is. And hooray for Yesss!"

"Well, anything for a top ten friend," you say as he puts you down. You give yourself an instant makeover. New dress, new hairdo.

When this guy hugs, everything wrinkles!

Turn to PAGE 255.

Surge Protector gazes at you, puzzled. "But why would that make your head shake . . . ? Oh, never mind. Move along, everybody, nothing to see here."

The crowd disperses. You mosey away to avoid seeming suspicious. As soon as Surge Protector is farther down the strip, you hurry back to the Wi-Fi socket.

You pace back and forth, anxiously waiting for Felix to return with Vanellope. Felix's wife, Calhoun, stomps over. "What were you thinking, sending Felix into uncharted territory?"

"I'm sorry, Calhoun," you tell her. "But I didn't send him in. He volunteered."

Calhoun's eyes narrow. "Somehow I don't think so." She thumps your chest with a finger, emphasizing each word. "More like he was **volun-*told*!**"

"I'm sure he's fine," you try to assure her. But after your experience in the Internet, you're not very convincing. It was a pretty crazy place.

She turns and faces the socket. She straightens her shoulders. "I'm going in."

And with that, she disappears into the socket.

Turn to PAGE 173.

"Just trying to help you in your search," he says. "I'm a search engine."

"Like those other guys," Ralph says, glowering at him.

"Yes, but I'm a bit more . . . a bit less . . . not so . . ." He clears his throat and starts over. "I'm **KnowsMore**. And I know more!"

"More what?" you ask.

That seems to perplex him.

"Never mind," you say. "We heard there's a place that people can buy—"

"Vegetables? Designer clothes? Discount furniture?" With each suggestion, an image pops up, until there are pictures piling on top of pictures on the counter. Big. Small. Black-and-white. Color. Sepia.

You glitch onto his counter and glare down at him. "Let me finish a sentence," you say, tugging your ponytail in frustration.

"Sorry," he says, shrinking away from you. "It's the **autofill** feature. Most people like it."

"Do we look like 'most people'?" Ralph demands, looming over KnowsMore.

KnowsMore studies you and then Ralph. He adjusts his bow tie. "Er . . . no. You do not. Look like other people."

"Let's try this again," you say. You speak very slowly and clearly, trying to remain patient. "My friend and I are in search of a steering wheel—"

KnowsMore opens his mouth. Ralph clamps his hand over it before any words can come out or any pictures can appear.

Turn to **PAGE 60**.

"Uh, nope. I—I didn't see anyone," you stammer. "It's not like Felix would ever do anything like that. He's the **Good Guy**, remember? He follows rules."

Surge Protector seems to be buying your story. Then Calhoun comes out of the Wi-Fi socket.

"I didn't see Felix in there anywhere!" she snaps.

You smack your forehead.

"What were *you* doing in there?" Surge Protector demands, taking a step toward Calhoun.

"Back off, blue boy," she snarls. "If my husband is in danger, it's up to me to go back in and get him."

"He went back in to look for you!" you tell her.

Her face goes soft and her eyes grow misty. "Why, that sweet buffoon."

As she turns to reenter the plug, you grab her arm. "I'm going with you."

Turn to **PAGE 235.**

You and Calhoun tiptoe into the **nursery**. A dozen cribs stand in rows, and a soft lullaby plays. "They're so cute," you whisper.

"Like little angels," Calhoun agrees.

You make your way down a row of cribs. As you turn, the hammer on your tool belt knocks a crib leg. The baby inside wakes up.

And starts crying.

Which wakes up the other babies.

Who start crying.

Which makes *you* want to start crying. . . .

Keep it together and get yourself to
PAGE 267.

"I know a guy we can talk to," you tell Calhoun. "He seems to know a lot. In fact, his name is **KnowsMore**."

You scan the area for KnowsMore's Search Bar. "There!" You point at his sign.

"We're on the move, soldier," Calhoun says.

A few minutes later you're approaching the kiosk. You see Felix there. At least one of your missing friends is accounted for.

"But that's not what I was asking," Felix is saying as you step up to the counter. Thousands of screens are open in front of him. Pictures on top of pictures. And KnowsMore keeps typing a mile a minute, autofilling like crazy.

"Felix!" Calhoun exclaims.

"Darling!" Felix greets his wife. "Why, hello there, Ralph. Good to see you."

"Uh, we just saw each other a minute ago, Felix," you tell him.

Your heart sinks. Felix and Calhoun found each other. But Vanellope is still missing.

Or is she?

Find out on **PAGE 205**.

The plug goes into the socket on the arcade side. On your side, the marquee sign above the socket lights up.

You peer at the neon letters, trying to figure out what they say.

"'**Whiff . . . whiffie'?**" you read, perplexed. "'**Wi . . . wifey'?** Hmm. It's either a Wiffle ball game or something about weddings."

Neither seems very interesting.

But as you glance around, everyone else seems mesmerized—Vanellope included.

Turn to **PAGE 106.**

YOU ARE GENE

NOTHING WOULD EVER GET DONE WITHOUT YOU, GENE. What are these people thinking? Sure, Vanellope's game is shut down for now, so it's fine for her to go gallivanting in that newfangled invention, the Internet. But what about your game, *Fix-It Felix, Jr.*? Without Ralph, it doesn't exactly run smoothly. But are any of these folks considering *that*?

"So, how are we going to deal with the missing Ralph issue?" you ask the group when everyone arrives in your penthouse, as they do most evenings.

"He's not missing," Felix says. "He's just in the Internet."

You roll your eyes. "Missing from the *game*," you say.

"Do we really need to worry about that now?" one of the ladies asks. "After all, the arcade is closed."

"We need to have a plan, in case Ralph and Vanellope don't come back by the time the arcade opens," you explain. "Those two have a tendency to get caught up in things. I wouldn't be surprised if Ralph is going to be MIA for a few days. Which could mean *our* game could be shut down."

The Nicelanders exchange worried glances.

Go to the NEXT PAGE.

"Remember," you continue, "we're a vintage game, too. If Litwak thinks we're broken, he just might have those junk dealers haul us away with *Sugar Rush*."

A gasp runs through the crowd. One Nicelander falls over in a faint.

"Didn't think of that, did ya?" you say.

"We can't let that happen!" a man shouts.

"We can't be shut down," a lady wails. "I just started a new quilting project!"

They burst into chatter, bordering on hysteria.

You hold up a hand to quiet them down. "Lucky for you folks, I already have an idea." You tap your forehead. "I'm always figuring the angles."

You gaze at their earnest faces, all eagerly waiting to hear your plan.

"I think we should hold auditions for a substitute Bad Guy," you say. "You know, kind of like having an understudy."

The room falls silent. They all stare at you.

Finally, Felix speaks up. "I think that's a brilliant suggestion," he says. "And I, for one, will be happy to help you."

Put your plan in motion on PAGE 129.

"So where do you think we should look?" you ask.

"I don't know," Vanellope says uncertainly. "None of those pictures look like the steering wheel from *Sugar Rush*."

She's right. But at least you've got a lead. "Maybe those are just the wheels they keep up front. After all, *Sugar Rush* is a pretty old game. No offense."

"None taken," Vanellope says. "And you may be right. So why don't you do the honor of picking where to go, Lord Big Butt." She gives you a bow.

"With pleasure, Lady Earwax." You bow back, then straighten up and study the pictures. *"Hmmmm."*

Do you tap on the image of a large wooden wheel? Turn to PAGE 208.

Or will the bicycle wheel take you where you want to go? Turn to PAGE 275.

A moment later you're deposited in an enormous bustling hall filled with booths.

And who's that right in front of you, scratching his butt? **"Ralph!"** you exclaim.

He turns. When he sees you, a huge smile spreads across his face. Then he frowns. Then he takes off running.

You smack your forehead. You forgot about the contest. He's trying to beat you to the steering wheel.

You chase after him. You glitch in and out of the crowd. He leads you to a booth displaying none other than your replacement wheel!

As Ralph reaches for it, you glitch up to the counter. Your fingers look tiny sitting on top of his massive hand.

You grin at him. He grins back.

"Call it a tie?" you ask.

"A-okay with me, little sister," he says.

Your heart is nearly bursting with happiness.

You found your wheel. You saved *Sugar Rush*.

And best of all—you don't have to do Ralph's laundry!

THE END.

You wait anxiously. You send messages all the time, but for some reason, this one was difficult. It's hard making the first move to reconnect, but you're glad you sent it.

Ding! A message pops up.

It's a reply from Perhaps!

So glad you reached out, you read. *On the one hand, you were very bossy, which I didn't like. On the other hand, perhaps you can't help being the way you are.*

Yep, sounds just like the Perhaps you used to know.

Glad you're not mad anymore, you type. *I was thinking, how about we get together offline? You know, IRL.*

There's a pause. You have a feeling she's weighing her options.

Wait for her response on PAGE 139.

You figure you can distract Surge Protector. You and Vanellope have done it often enough. You're practically experts at getting around him and his watchful gaze.

You put on your best **worried** face and rush up to him. "Hey, Surge, are we glad to see you! We want to report some malfeasance over there."

Surge frowns and studies you and Vanellope. She arranges her features into a very sincere concerned expression. If you didn't know she was playacting, you'd be worried yourself. "Yeah, we saw some undesirables causing a real **donnybrook** over there."

Surge snaps to attention. "A malfeasance-based donny-brook? Oh, heck no. Not on my watch. Appreciate the tip!" He rushes away.

You and Vanellope high-five. Your plan worked!

Travel to a brand-new world on PAGE 74.

You and Ralph are suddenly surrounded by a group of **netizens**. Each carries a portable keyboard.

"Search? I can help with that," the little fellow wearing a headset says.

"I have all the answers," says another netizen with large glasses.

"My returns are the best!" says a woman standing near a cart.

"Me! Me! Pick me!" shouts a man with a search bar sign.

"I guess these folks can help," Ralph says.

"Of course we can," one of them says. "We're search engines. We help people find what they want to find, go where they want to go."

You step up to the man with the search bar, ignoring the other search engines crowding around you. "How does this work?" you ask him.

"Just type in what you're looking for." He holds out his keyboard.

Seems easy enough. "Okay." You reach for the keyboard.

But before you can even touch the keys, a scrawny dude comes out of nowhere. He shoves the sign he's carrying right in front of you. You throw out your hand to keep from falling over. The minute your hand touches his sign, music blares—and you're whisked somewhere else!

Find out where on **PAGE 43**.

"*I am Bad. And that's good,*" you and the group of Bad Guys chant together. "*I will never be Good. And that's not bad. There's no one I'd rather be than me.*"

You're at a weekly **Bad-Anon** meeting, a support group for arcade game villains. They talk about what it's like never to win medals and to have everyone hate you. You found it pretty helpful, back before you met Vanellope. This chant closes every meeting.

"Before you all go," you say as the group prepares to leave, "I have an announcement. A request. A . . . an idea to run by you."

"Which is it?" Shinobi, the masked ninja, asks.

"Let's call it an idea for a request that I'm announcing," you reply.

"Go ahead, Ralph," one of your fellow Bad Guys encourages.

"So, here's the thing," you say, unsure how the group of Bad Guys will respond. "*Sugar Rush* has never had any Bad Guys. I thought it would add a little excitement if some of us joined that game."

They glance at each other. You can tell they're not exactly brimming with enthusiasm.

Turn to PAGE 6.

A moment later, Felix scrambles out of the socket. "My, my, my," he says. "That is some **exciting** place." He's holding a dripping ice-cream cone.

"Where's Vanellope?" you demand.

"Sorry, Ralph. I didn't see Vanellope. I called and called." Felix licks his ice-cream cone. "Then I asked this little fellow called KnowsMore if he knew how I could make a missing person's report. A form popped up. I started to write Vanellope's name, but as soon as I put in the first letters, the word *vanilla* appeared. KnowsMore called that 'autofill.'"

He holds up the ice-cream cone. "Anyhoo, that's how I wound up in the Fifty Flavor franchise. And suddenly, I was holding a vanilla ice-cream cone." He takes another lick. "Pretty tasty, too. It has little bits of real vanilla beans and—"

"Felix! I don't care about the ice cream. I care about finding Vanellope!"

Turn to **PAGE 221.**

You're fascinated *and* horrified. Zombie uses his newly detached leg to smash a brick with impressive force. The brick shatters, but Zombie shatters along with it. His head falls and lands at your feet.

"Give me another shot," Zombie's head begs. "I just need a minute to put myself back together."

You bang the clipboard on the table, startling Felix. You fling up your hands. **"This is ridiculous!"**

"Now, now," Felix says. "Just take a deep breath. We'll figure it out."

You shake your head as you sit back down.

You're not sure what to do.

Should you give up on this audition idea?
Go to PAGE 33.

Or should you hold some more auditions?
Go to PAGE 273.

You click on an old, old photo of yourself. You flash back to a time before you understood the proper way to take a **selfie**, could use filters, or to be honest, understood anything about style.

"C'mon, Yesss," you say to encourage yourself, "I bet you can find lots of interesting things in the Internet."

You sign on and find an intriguing site. "Well, that place looks interesting."

Go to the NEXT PAGE.

You luck out on your very first try. The site you visit is called **OhMyDisney**, and there's so much to see! You have fun with the quizzes. You listen to music. You try out fashion ideas. You experiment with recipes.

But even better, you have lots of things to talk about with other netizens. You have so much in common with them, since they spend time at OhMyDisney, too. You start seeing movies together. You exchange ideas about what you see on the site. You start to develop opinions of your own. Opinions that others respect!

This Internet is fabulous! you decide. You study everything you can about it. You learn how to make your own videos, generate your own GIFs, and make things go viral.

Thanks to the Internet, your life as a lonely outsider has come to . . .

AN END.

A few minutes later, a video you shoot of Ralph is blasted all over the Internet. His image crying out, "Where are you, Vanellope?" plays in a continuous loop on a number of very popular video sites.

"Now we just sit back and wait," you tell Ralph.

He points at the screen. "Do I really look like that?"

Before you can answer, a new video pops up on one of your screens.

"It's Vanellope!" Ralph cries.

She's moving her mouth, but you can't hear anything. "I think she's using a video chat. Hang on."

You click a few buttons, and in moments Vanellope's voice comes through your speakers loud and clear. "Yo! Ralph! What's happening! How'd you get in a video?"

Ralph turns to you, his expression full of admiration. "Lady, you are *good*."

You shrug modestly. "Hey, Internet is what I do." You swing around your console so he can speak into it. "Go ahead. She'll hear you."

"I got the steering wheel!" Ralph says. "And I made a cool new friend!"

Awww. You're blushing again.

Turn to PAGE 256.

Everyone from *Sugar Rush* swarms through the plug and into Game Central Station.

Surge Protector is doing his usual security patrol of the socket strip. He startles, then waves his arms back and forth. "No running! Stop running!" he shouts. "What are you doing out of your game, for Peter's sake? The arcade's open!"

"*Sugar Rush* is getting unplugged," you explain.

The *Sugar Rush* drivers shout and wail, making a racket. You feel terrible. Without the steering wheel, their game may be gone for good! Well, for *bad*, actually. *Really* bad.

"Where are we supposed to go?" Vanellope asks. She glitches, but not in the way you've seen her glitch before—this is different.

You realize she feels responsible for the well-being of the citizens of her game, and it's *her* broken steering wheel that shut things down.

"Stay here, I guess, until the arcade closes," Surge Protector says. "Then we'll figure out where the heck we're gonna put you." He glares at you. "And, Ralph, get back to your game!"

"But—" you begin to protest.

Vanellope tugs your finger. "Go ahead," she tells you. "We'll be okay for now."

You trudge back to your game, but the minute the arcade closes, you rush back to Game Central Station. By the time you arrive, they've already worked out a temporary plan. The drivers are taking up temporary residence in *Fix-It Felix, Jr.* Some of the drivers seem kind of down about it, but you're pretty excited about your plans for you and Vanellope.

Turn to **PAGE 115**.

You smack your forehead. Why didn't you think of this before? "You should try *my* game!"

You bring her into *Fix-It Felix, Jr.* "As you may have heard," you tell the Nicelanders you have gathered outside their big building, "*Sugar Rush* is having a wee bit of a problem."

The sympathetic murmurs give you confidence that they'll agree to your plan. "So I decided to bring Vanellope into our game."

They stare at you silently. Finally, Felix raises his hand.

"Yes, Felix?" you say.

"I'm sure you know we were all just devastated to hear the news," he says. Everyone nods sadly. "And I, for one, just love how devoted you are to your friend." The Nicelanders all nod warmly. "But I'm wondering—what exactly will Vanellope *do*?"

Now all the Nicelanders look at you with wondering expressions.

"Well, now," you say, "I haven't actually worked that—"

"I'm Ralph's assistant!" Vanellope pipes up.

"You are?" you say. "That's right! You are!"

The Nicelanders exchange glances. "If you think she can do it, I say, why not?" Felix says.

"Let's give it a trial run!" Vanellope says.

Go to the NEXT PAGE.

"You know how this game works, right?" you ask Vanellope.

"Sure," she says. "You smash up the building. Felix fixes it with his magic hammer."

She doesn't sound all that enthusiastic. "Well, it's a little more complicated than that," you say.

"There *is* some **strategy** involved," Felix adds. You can tell he's a bit miffed by Vanellope's dismissive attitude. "I have to watch out for falling bricks, and the flying geese. I have to collect pies. . . ."

"And it takes all of us to throw Ralph off the building," Gene chimes in.

"Yeah," you say, "not just *anyone* could take my place."

"Er, about that." Vanellope tugs your sleeve and pulls you to a quiet spot behind the building.

Find out what's on her mind on PAGE 32.

This is it! The home stretch! The teams have completed their individual laps and are racing toward the finish line together.

You bring down your flag as all five members of Minty's team cross the finish line. **"We have a winning team!"** you announce over the loudspeakers.

The drivers from Minty's team jump out of their karts squealing and cheering. You join them on the track.

"That was so much fun!" Minty gushes. She has her arms slung across the shoulders of her teammates. All of them grin from ear to ear.

"Somehow it feels even more exciting to win as a *team*," Swizzle says.

"Even with Vanellope playing next time," Taffyta adds, "the group effort means she's not *always* going to win! That gives the rest of us a chance."

You smile proudly. This was a good idea. Good for morale. Good for the game. You haven't seen the drivers this jazzed in, well, you don't know how long. And their renewed energy sparks yours.

"Let's race again!" you say. "This time, Minty, you're the judge."

She takes the flag from you. "Everybody," she announces, "swap teams."

You have a feeling there are going to be many relay races from now on. You're already thinking of ways to keep them challenging. You'd love to get Ralph in on the action.

Oh, the possibilities! You don't have to worry about being bored ever again.

THE END.

You gently pick up the egg. It looks so fragile. On your way home, you ask everyone you meet if they lost an egg. Or if they know what game it's from. You get the same answers over and over. "Not my egg" and "Not a clue." You'll have to wait until it hatches to discover where it belongs.

At home, you gently lay the egg on the kitchen counter. Your wife, Calhoun, joins you. "Um . . .?" She tips her head toward the egg, waiting for an explanation.

"I found it all alone in Game Central Station," you explain. "I couldn't just leave it there."

She smiles warmly. "Of course you couldn't. **Softie.**"

You and Calhoun carefully lower yourselves to the stools. You both stare at the egg.

"When do you think it's going to hatch?" you whisper.

"No idea," Calhoun murmurs.

Go to the NEXT PAGE.

You and Calhoun move carefully around the egg as you go about your lives, keeping a watchful eye on it. The next day, Gene stops by to let you know that Vanellope and Ralph have returned. They found the replacement steering wheel and *Sugar Rush* will be plugged back in.

"That's great," you say, your eyes still on the egg.

"Tomorrow's a workday," Calhoun reminds you after Gene leaves. "What are we going to do with the egg?"

"Gosh, I don't know," you say. "Both of our games are much too dangerous for the little critter. It could get broken so easily."

Suddenly, the egg wiggles. You and Calhoun both gasp.

You hear a teeny tapping sound coming from inside the egg. A tiny little crack appears in the shell. You grip Calhoun's hand. You can't wait to see what will emerge!

You hear more pecking inside the egg, and soon you can see a snout.

"That doesn't look much like a bird," Calhoun comments.

The shell breaks completely and your eyes widen.

"It's a baby stegosaurus!" you exclaim.

Turn to *PAGE 42.*

The pod releases you on some kind of viewing platform. You take one step forward and stop. You gasp. You can't believe what you're seeing.

"This place is *amazing*!" you exclaim.

Spread out in front of you is a vast world unlike anything you've ever seen. Tall buildings connect to a transport system that zips riders to their destinations in an instant. Multicolored signs scream for your attention—in some cases *literally*! Music plays, lights blink on and off, and everywhere you look *something* is happening. And happening *fast*!

Go to the **NEXT PAGE.**

You fling out your arms wide. "I want to go everywhere!" you declare.

Ralph lands with a thump and a grunt beside you. He slowly picks himself up and backs away from the balcony ledge. **"Whoa."** He covers his eyes. **"Dizzy."**

"Isn't it incredible?" You drag him back to the edge of the balcony. You peel his fingers away from his face. "Hang on to the railing. You'll be fine."

He clutches the railing.

"Just don't look down," you caution him.

He looks down.

And stumbles backward again.

"I told you not to look down." You roll your eyes at him.

Go to the NEXT PAGE.

You glitch up onto the balcony railing for a better view. You marvel at all the activity below you.

"Don't do that!" Ralph hurries back to the balcony.

"Aw, no worries, big dude," you tell him as he lifts you down from the railing. "I'd have **glitched** if I thought I might fall."

He mops his forehead. "I can see why Surge Protector warned us about this place."

You look up at him, surprised. "Really? I think it's beautiful." You spot an escalator leading down to the main floor. "And we're going to go explore it!"

"We are?" Ralph asks. He sighs. "Of course we are."

"No wonder those kids thought they could find a *Sugar Rush* steering wheel here," you tell Ralph as you ride the escalator. "This place must have everything!"

Turn to **PAGE 145.**

You've got to catch up with Vanellope and tell her your idea. You hop the tram out of your game to Game Central Station.

There's just one **problem**: you don't know where Vanellope went.

You step on top of a bench, trying to get a better view of the crowded, enormous space. She could have gone back to *Sugar Rush*. She wouldn't be able to go inside, since it's been unplugged. But maybe she wanted to see it one last time.

But when you get to the game, there's no one around.

"If my game was about to go out of commission, where would I go?" you murmur.

That's a no-brainer. If *Fix-It Felix, Jr.* was about to be put out to pasture, you'd go hang out with your best friend. Vanellope. In *Sugar Rush*.

But she just *left* your game. The fact that she couldn't turn to you for comfort in her time of distress seriously bums you out.

Still . . . she said she needed some alone time. Maybe she's had enough by now and has returned to *Fix-It Felix, Jr.*

Or maybe she never left. Maybe she just didn't want to be on top of that building.

Go back to your game on PAGE 125.

You and Vanellope tumble out of the game. You try not to breathe as you pluck a dirty diaper off your arm. You hurl it back into the game.

"Yuck, yuck, yuck!" Vanellope wriggles with disgust.

You point at her face. "Um, you've got some mashed peas on your nose."

She swipes at her face. "And you've got a rattle dangling from your overalls."

You and Vanellope wash up as best you can in one of the enormous fountains in Game Central Station.

"I know *Baby Bonanza* wasn't exactly your cup of tea—" you begin.

Vanellope snorts. "Or baby formula."

"But I don't think we should give up on finding you another game. Just in case."

Vanellope frowns, considering. She dries her face on your overalls, then steps back to look up at you. "You know, you kinda had the right idea."

"I did?" You brighten. "I mean, of course I did."

Go to the NEXT PAGE.

"Your choice of game was terrible," Vanellope continues. "Like, the worst idea ever. On a top ten list of horrible, awful—"

You hold up a hand to interrupt her. "I get the point. *Baby Bonanza*. **Bad**."

"But if we have to give up *Sugar Rush*, there must be other games we can join."

You grin broadly. "That's the ticket!"

She plops down onto the side of the fountain. "But what other racing games are there in Game Central Station?"

You sit down beside her. "Expand your horizons! Other kinds of games are fun, too. You don't have to only think of racing games."

"I don't know. . . ."

"C'mon." You stand, grab her hand, and pull her to her feet. "We've got three popular games right here. Which do you want to try?"

She frowns and then shrugs. "I don't know. You pick."

You heard Vanellope. Choose!

Should you check out **Aliens Attack** *on* **PAGE 36**?

Or try **Hero's Duty.** *That's the game Felix's wife, Calhoun, is in. It's on* **PAGE 28**.

Or maybe **Bust a Move** *on* **PAGE 100**.

Or should you bring her into your game, **Fix-It Felix, Jr.,** *on* **PAGE 179**?

You pass a row of pictures of people. Could that be it? Do the pictures need to be arranged by type? Many have the phrase "Best Friends Forever" or "BFF" under them.

You reach out to pluck one of the pictures from the wall.

"You! Cut it out!"

You freeze, your hand still reaching for the photo of the best friends hugging. "Me?"

"Quit messing with the pictures. The users won't be able to find them again!"

Another guard arrives. "We've got a problem," he tells the others. "Rows four and five have been completely rearranged."

"And we have entire categories mixed together," another one says. "Sunrises with shoes!"

Uh-oh. Sounds like your collection of pink pictures.

Before they can figure out that you're the one behind the mess, walk as innocently as possible to PAGE 78.

"You're acting kind of **weird**, Princess Vanny," she says. "Come on. We should be getting to the starting line. To, you know, *not* start."

You and red-haired Taffyta stroll toward the starting point of the race. You notice she's in no hurry. You suppose if they're not doing much driving, there probably isn't an actual race.

"Hey, what happened to the gumdrop obstacle course?" you ask.

"The what?" Taffyta stops and puts her hand on your forehead. "Are you okay? Do you have a fever or something?"

You swat away her hand. "I'm fine."

"Minty and Crumbelina are already there," Taffyta says. "Wait a sec. Who's that other . . . ?"

And now it's gonna get interesting, you think.

Turn to PAGE 49.

"Wait for me, kid!" you shout. The moment your big feet hit the platform, a pod forms around you, too. It's a tight fit.

With a **whoosh**, your pod catapults you through miles of cable. You bellow in terror. Ahead, you can hear Vanellope whooping with delight.

"Isn't this great?!" she calls.

"No, it is *not*!" you bellow. You're so squished inside your pod your nose is pressed flat against the front window and your knees squeeze against your belly.

Thankfully, the pod stops and its doors burst open. You fall out onto your face in front of Vanellope.

You get to your feet and try to loosen your sore muscles.

"Sweet mother of monkey milk," Vanellope murmurs.

What has her so mesmerized? You rub your aching neck. You look up. "Holy cow, kid," you say. "I don't think we're in Litwak's anymore."

You stand on a viewing platform. Before you, as far as your eyes can see, are magical-looking island cities connected by shining superhighways. Each seems to be its own unique world. You hear music but can't figure out where it's coming from. There are signs everywhere and lots of blinking lights. There's so much activity it's almost overwhelming. You're staring at pure chaos.

"Whoa," Vanellope breathes.

"Okay, there's got to be loads of steering wheels out there," you say.

"Yeah. But how are we going to find the one we **need**?"

"Don't worry, little sister. We'll figure it out."

Go to the NEXT PAGE.

"Look at all the people!" Vanellope points down to the street. "They must live here."

You watch the colorful crowds go about their busy day. Some ride in snazzy-looking vehicles, others stroll, and still others hop on and off moving sidewalks. You get the sense that everything here is in constant motion. "The citizens of the Internet," you say.

"Netizens!" Vanellope says.

"Netizens," you repeat. "I like it."

"So whaddya say," she says, her eyes twinkling. "Shall we go introduce ourselves to some netizens?"

"I think we shall!" you say.

Go to the NEXT PAGE.

Vanellope twirls around and charges ahead. "Over here!" she calls. You watch her disappear down an escalator.

You hurry to catch up. You have a feeling that a person could get lost forever in this Internet place.

You reach the crowded street level. You're moving so fast trying to keep Vanellope in sight you run into someone. "Sorry, sorry," you say. **"Whaaa?"**

You stare as the square-headed, flat-looking fellow breaks apart into zeros and ones. *Binary code*, you realize. The numbers float away, then burst like bubbles.

"Don't worry," a netizen tells you. He seems to be sorting mail. "That was just an avatar. You didn't really hurt anyone."

"An avatar?" you ask.

"See, out there"—he gestures with his envelopes up to the spot where you and Vanellope entered—"there's a human online. That human has a representative here. An avatar."

"So I didn't hurt the human?" you ask.

"Nah," the guy says. "The human will just log back on."

You only understood about half of what this mailman said, but the important thing is that you didn't hurt anyone.

Go to the NEXT PAGE.

"Thanks," you tell him. You glance around.

Oh, no. You can't see Vanellope anywhere. "Say, have you seen a girl about yea high?" You hold out your hand, demonstrating. "Ponytail?"

"Thattaway" He points an envelope to the right.

You hurry along and spot Vanellope heading toward a kiosk. You read the sign above the counter: THE SEARCH BAR. Below the sign stands a small fellow. He wears big glasses and a cap and gown like kids graduating from college wear.

You reach Vanellope just as she steps up to the counter. "Good afternoon, KnowsMore," she says, reading his name tag.

"Welcome to the Search Bar," KnowsMore replies. He pushes his glasses up and squints at you and Vanellope. "What can KnowsMore help you find today?"

"My fellow adventurer and I are searching for something," you say.

As soon as the word *search* comes out of your mouth, you're surrounded.

Turn to PAGE 64.

YOU ARE VANELLOPE

LIFE IS SWEET IN YOUR GAME *SUGAR RUSH*.
Driving through lollipop forests with the wind bouncing your ponytail, accelerating up to the crest of a donut hill, then barreling down the frosted side. But if you're super-duper honest with yourself, it could be sweeter.

It's true that things are a whole lot better for you ever since you and that goofball Ralph from the game *Fix-It Felix, Jr.* became besties. You embraced your code, even though it made you different. Now everyone in *Sugar Rush* is totally on your side. They accept you as the beautiful, unique glitch you are.

There's just one problem: you're kinda **bored**.

Driving is in your blood. It's who you are. But the *Sugar Rush* race just doesn't challenge you anymore.

What can you do about it, though? A track is a track. *Or is it?*

You shake your head. "Of course it is," you tell yourself. Silly question.

Still, it gets you thinking. What if you changed things?

If you want to alter the game, go to **PAGE 231.**
If you figure you should leave well enough alone, turn to **PAGE 280.**

"Whoa!" you exclaim. The candy karts zoom around you, your hair flying and overalls flapping in the breeze they create.

"Off-road!" you hear Vanellope shout.

Instantly, the line of karts breaks up and the karts scatter. They leave the track.

You don't believe it! They're going after the Bad Guys.

Vanellope has her sights on Zombie. He has finished chopping down trees and is now loitering over by the chocolate pond. Clearly, he figures his appearance alone is enough to frighten a *Sugar Rush* driver.

He's never met Vanellope.

She revs her engine. He glances up, then startles. She drives straight toward him. He scrambles backward, trying to put distance between them without taking his eyes off her.

She drives right into the chocolate pond. He trips and falls just as she makes a sharp turn. Her wheels screech and chocolate goes flying. She races away, leaving Zombie completely drenched in chocolate—and humiliation.

Turn to **PAGE 89**.

You can see KnowsMore is on the fence. "C'mon, KnowsMore," you plead. "Help a girl out in her pursuit of knowledge. Isn't that like, your **mission**?"

That gets him.

"I'll see what I can do." He peers at each image, then types on his keyboard.

You flex your fingers. You can't wait to wrap them around those steering wheels!

"Hmmm. They're each being sold on different websites," he says. "That means you'd have to visit each one separately."

"Um, I don't know if we have time to visit each place," Ralph warns. "Clock's ticking."

You know he's right. Disappointment floods through you.

"How about this," Ralph offers. "KnowsMore helps me snag that steering wheel. And while I do that, you go race."

"Really?" You beam. He must realize how badly you want to see the earlier versions of *Sugar Rush*. "I'll only play *one* of the games. That way we'll for sure get you back to your game before there's any trouble."

You and Ralph smile at each other.

Turn to PAGE 151.

Turn to PAGE 151.

Now you notice that there are a few guards posted among the gazillion images. You suppose you could ask one of the guards how to play, but that feels like it would be cheating.

You snap your fingers. "Colors!"

You race through the rows of images, grabbing all the pink ones. You hurl them at a wall and step back. Pink flowers, sunsets, handbags, dresses, and sunrises hang in front of you. You glance around. **Nothing happens.** No bells, no confetti, and certainly no medals. "Guess that's not it."

You notice a few guards are talking together. One of them points at you.

"Yeah, yeah, yeah," you call. "I'll get it in a minute. Just give me another shot."

Try again on PAGE 190.

"Here we go!" You shout with excitement. A new plug to enter! You wonder what you'll find.

Ralph looks a little nervous. "Don't worry, King Klutz," you tell him. "It'll be great!"

You and Ralph step onto the moving sidewalk that will take you up through the plug. You **frown** when you arrive at your destination.

"This is what Surge Protector was so afraid of?" You gaze around the cavernous space.

"Why?"

"Maybe he's afraid of big empty places?" Ralph suggests.

"There's nothing here," you say, confused. "Why would those kids say the steering wheel is here?"

You slump in despair. You were so certain you'd be able to save your game.

Drag yourself to **PAGE 270**.

"Okay," you tell the assembled Bad Guys. "When I count to three, we'll charge in together. That will be the **first surprise**."

The Bad Guys all nod. "Sounds good," Cyborg says.

"Then position yourselves throughout the game," you instruct them. "They'll have already seen you, so they'll know you're in there. That will keep 'em on their toes."

More nods and grunts of approval.

"Jump out at the drivers as they speed by," you continue. "Maybe growl or wail or smash something. Whatever your thing is. Maybe chase them down the tracks. You know the drill. You're all professionals."

You hand out the dark glasses for the Bad Guys who aren't used to bright lights and vivid colors. You hold a finger to your lips for silence, then gesture for them to follow you into the game. You all creep into position, just behind a stand of cotton candy bushes.

Go to the NEXT PAGE.

You know Vanellope's game nearly as well as your own. Sour Bill gives the signal for the race to begin. Only this time, he makes a big show of waving the flag around to be sure you and your Bad Guys know it's time to put your plan into action.

Sour Bill finishes his very dramatic swishing and swashing of the flag. He holds it high above his round green head.

"**Now!**" you shout.

You and your Bad Guys rush the track, bellowing, hollering, and making a general racket.

The drivers shriek—including Vanellope, you're proud to say.

Turn to PAGE 52.

You're itching to try those alternate tracks. You wonder what the differences might be. Maybe there are things in those versions you can incorporate into *your Sugar Rush*.

"Can we go play the games?" you ask KnowsMore.

"Of course. Once you buy them, you can do anything with them. Turn them into lamps if you want."

"Lamps?" Ralph asks.

He shrugs. "Some people will turn pretty much anything into a lamp. Or a planter. Lots of planters being sold on Etsy."

"Ooo-kay." This guy may know a lot, but not all of it makes much sense.

"But we don't want to buy the games," Ralph reminds you. "We just want a steering wheel."

Dang. And you'd really like to see how those versions compare with yours. Then you have an idea. "How about a test drive?" you ask. "After all, you'd never buy a car if you didn't try it out first."

"I don't know . . ." KnowsMore says.

"And here I thought you knew everything," you say.

"Well . . ."

"Aw, KnowsMore," you wheedle. "I'm sure you can figure out a way. After all, you *know more*." You elbow Ralph. "Amiright?"

Go to **PAGE 198**.

"Love it!" Minty cries.

You grin at her. You're not surprised she's the first person to go for your idea. She almost never makes it into the top three in any race.

Taffyta shrugs. "I'm willing." She sounds a bit more reluctant. Of all the drivers, she's the only one who ever comes close to beating you.

Finally, everyone agrees to play the game as a relay race. **Once.**

"Here's how it will go," you announce. "We form teams. Each team decides the order of the drivers. Each driver will complete one lap. Once they return to the starting line, the next driver on the team goes. Once all team members have completed a lap, they *all* drive to the finish line. The team that gets all its players across the finish line first will be declared the winner!"

There's a burst of conversation. *They're really excited*, you observe with satisfaction. Suddenly, several drivers rush over to you. "We want you on our team," one shouts. "No, Vanellope should be on our team," someone else insists.

Uh-oh. You wanted this to be a *less* competitive version of the game. Since you're the best driver, they all want you on their teams.

Sure, it's nice to be acknowledged this way, but you need to find a solution. Or this idea will tank before you even try it.

Turn to **PAGE 12.**

"Sir Burps-a-Lot!"

You whirl around. **"Vanellope!"** you cheer.

She rushes toward you. And from the gleeful expression on her face, you think her news is good.

"I found the wheel!" she cries. "And it's on its way to Litwak's Family Fun Center even as we speak."

"This calls for high—"

"Chairs?" KnowsMore suggests. "School?"

"Stop autofilling!" you, Felix, Calhoun, and Vanellope shout together.

"Fives?" KnowsMore asks weakly.

You're about to smash KnowsMore's keyboard when you stop yourself.

"Actually, come to think of it, that's exactly what I was going to say. High fives all around."

KnowsMore looks relieved. You all slap hands, and you even include KnowsMore.

"Everyone hold hands," you instruct. "We're not leaving anyone behind this time."

Vanellope squeezes your hand. "As if that could ever really happen."

You grin. You're so glad it all worked out in . . .

THE END.

You whirl around to face Calhoun. "Looky here!" you say. "I think I'm onto something. Try it."

Calhoun leans into the crib in front of her and picks up the kicking and sputtering infant. Again: instant silence.

"It's like a **superpower**," she says in awe. Then she snaps out of it and demands, "But what about all these others? We don't have enough arms to pick up all of them!"

"That is a puzzler," you say, bouncing the baby in your arms as you pace beside the cribs. Your heart breaks to see all their little scrunched-up faces.

And your ears ache from all the screeching!

Go to the NEXT PAGE.

A few moments later, you and Calhoun sit on the floor, surrounded by babies.

Happy, giggling, gurgling babies.

"You are a **genius**," Calhoun says. "Putting all the little critters into a pile so they could play with us and each other. Pure genius."

"Having them all together does seem to make them happy," you say. "But it was your idea to check their diapers and to give them bottles."

"Well, I know from experience with my soldiers that being hungry can make a person moody," Calhoun says, bouncing a happy baby on her lap. "And they all know they have to have on clean underwear before suiting up."

"Looks like you managed just fine."

You look up to see Miss Nanny beaming in the doorway. "By jiminy, I think we did," you say.

"Say," she says as she takes off her coat, "would you two like jobs here? We can always use good people with excellent baby skills."

"We're very glad we could help out," you say. "But we're needed in our own games."

Once you and Calhoun are out of the game, you turn to each other. "Fighting cy-bugs is a cakewalk compared to taking care of babies," Calhoun says.

"Those babies wore me out more than Ralph ever could," you say.

You're glad you helped Miss Nanny. But you're very glad to be heading back to your own games. And you're looking forward to a well-earned nap!

THE END.

As soon as you tap the picture, a pod appears, whisking you and Vanellope to a new place. When you arrive, you discover it's an **online game**—one that takes place on some kind of large wooden ship.

"Welcome to the HMS *Winthrop*," a netizen dressed in an old-fashioned sailor uniform greets you. He stands in front of a room-size picture of a ship. In front of it sits the large steering wheel you selected back at KnowsMore's Search Bar. You notice a large standing compass, a few barrels, and other nautical-type things stashed around the space.

"Howdy!" you reply as you scan the area.

"Greetings and salutations," Vanellope says.

You give her a quizzical look.

She shrugs. "I thought it sounded polite and old-fashioned."

"Where can I direct you?" The sailor strides up to a large board with a list. "You've come in through one of our back doors. Would you like to start again at the beginning?"

"What is this place?" you ask.

"This is the HMS *Winthrop*, a nineteenth-century schooner," the sailor says. "Best in the fleet. It was in service from—"

"No," you interrupt. "*This* place." You point at the floor. "Specifically."

Turn to PAGE 236.

A massive hand breaks through the white wall. You'd know that hammer-like fist anywhere. "Ralph!" you cry. "Get me outta here!"

His fingers grip your collar and he yanks you right out of wherever you are.

You look around. You're back on the main floor of the Internet hub. One of the search engines still holds out his keyboard.

"What happened? Where'd I go?" you ask.

"You fell into a **pop-up ad**," he tells you. He scowls. "Those pop-ups. They're always trying to divert users into their ads. I'm going to need to file a complaint about our Pop-Up Blocker. He's supposed to keep that from happening."

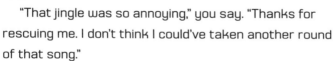

"Pop-Up Blocker?" you repeat.

"He's been slacking off," the search engine continues. "I think maybe he's old code. Needs an upgrade."

"That jingle was so annoying," you say. "Thanks for rescuing me. I don't think I could've taken another round of that song."

Go to the **NEXT PAGE**.

"Now about that search . . . ?" The search engine holds the **keyboard** out again.

You're surrounded again.

"We don't have pop-ups!" the search engine with the glasses shouts. "Your search is safe with us!"

"We're faster and more targeted!" another shouts.

"We're the best. The best! The best!"

They're closing in. Your nerves are on edge from those dancing dishes. Now this?

Turn to **PAGE 284.**

"Help!" you shout. You never learned to swim!

It takes five sailors huffing and puffing to haul you out of the water, using a giant net. They dump you onto the deck. You lie sprawled there, sputtering.

"You looked like a **ginormous fish** in that net," Vanellope teases.

"Felt like one, too. Still do." You stand and shake yourself, spraying water everywhere.

"Hey!" Vanellope yelps. "You're getting me all wet."

The captain strides toward you. "You two! I can't have such undisciplined menaces on my ship. We are dropping you off at the first sight of land."

"But how will we get home?" you ask.

"Not my problem," he growls.

Go to **PAGE 146**.

You wander into the woods, skirting past the disguised train station, and discover a path running alongside a brook.

You hear **laughter** up ahead. You wonder who you're going to meet!

You peek between two thick bushes. Your mouth drops open.

A dragon lies sunning itself on a big flat rock. A squat troll sits on another rock, his big hairy feet dangling in the water. A tiny winged fairy flits between them.

"So then I said," the troll is saying, "then I said . . ." He starts laughing and can't finish the sentence.

"Elmer," the dragon says, chuckling, "I have a feeling if you ever manage to get out your story, it won't be anywhere near as funny as you think it is."

Elmer the troll splashes water at the dragon. The fairy giggles. It sounds like bells.

"Hey!" the dragon complains. But you can tell he's not really mad. They all seem like good friends.

Here's your chance to make some new friends yourself!

Go to the NEXT PAGE.

You stride out of the bushes. "Hello, there!"

The dragon startles, blowing fire from his mouth. The troll falls off his rock into the stream with a loud splash. The fairy flies straight at you.

"Hey!" You cover your head and duck. You feel something land on your shoulder. It's the fairy.

"What are you doing, coming here and scaring folks like that?" she scolds.

"I didn't mean to," you say. "I just wanted to say hello."

The troll drags himself out of the stream. He shakes like a dog, spraying water everywhere.

"Cut it out!" the dragon yelps. "You're getting me all wet!"

"Looks like we have a fake elf among us," the fairy announces from her perch on your shoulder.

"How'd you know I'm fake?" you ask.

She tweaks your nose. "We know the difference between real magical creatures and visitors!"

"Don't worry," the troll says, "the avatars will never guess."

They don't seem mad. Phew.

Go to the NEXT PAGE.

You spend the most amazing day with your new magical friends. The troll takes you to a tavern where you play card games. The fairy introduces you to talking flowers. You go for a ride on the dragon's back. You even meet a group of real elves who invite you to join them in some serious pranking.

You can't wait to tell Ralph all about it!

Finally, you decide it's time to go back home. After all, Ralph must have found the steering wheel by now. And there's no *Sugar Rush* without you!

On the train ride back, groups of excited but exhausted avatars compare notes and tell stories. You have plenty of your own stories to tell.

You can't wait to return to this place. You're definitely going to bring Ralph next time. You think he'd make a perfect **ogre**!

THE END.

You're excited to see all the different kinds of ships when you and Vanellope arrive at a port. Dozens of impressive sailing ships are docked in a row. A number of avatars—online representatives of humans—stroll along the pier, too. They read plaques posted along the pier, walk up the gangplanks, and take pictures on board. Everyone seems to be having a wonderful time.

"Cool ships," Vanellope says. "You think they ever race them?"

"We could ask," you say. "But they don't look like they go very fast."

"Excuse me." A boy avatar wearing a school uniform approaches you. "Can you tell me what kind of ship that is?" He points to the ship in front of you with a pencil.

"Well, let's see," you say. You don't really want to admit you don't know.

You glance at Vanellope. *Uh-oh.* She has an impish look on her face that you know all too well: her prank face.

"I do believe that's a Von Schweetz," she says seriously. "Fastest ship in the fleet."

"I do believe you're wrong, madam." You point at a ship farther down the pier. "That lovely scow yonder is the fastest ship. The Ralph-a-Rama."

Try to keep from laughing on **PAGE 239.**

"If I knew that being a swabbie meant we had to mop the floor, I wouldn't have picked it," you complain. You lift your mop and swoosh it along the deck.

"At least your stomach has calmed down," Vanellope says. She pushes her ponytail out of her face and dunks her mop into the bucket of water. "But yeah. This sailor's life isn't for me."

"You, there," a shipmate calls. "Be sure you **swab the poop**."

You and Vanellope gape at each other, then burst out laughing.

"Swab . . . swab the . . . the *poop*?" Vanellope falls over, guffawing.

"Th-that can't mean what we think it means," you say, wiping tears of laughter from your eyes.

"Stop being idiots," the mate scolds you. "You know the poop deck is at the back of the ship. The highest spot on the deck." He shakes his head and points. "It forms the roof of the cabin. The *captain's* cabin," he adds for emphasis.

"R-right," you say, trying to get control of yourself. "Captain's roof."

You pick up the mop and bucket while Vanellope continues to giggle.

Just then, the fellow up in the crow's nest cries out, "Pirates!"

Pirates?

Go to the NEXT PAGE.

"Please, oh, please can we join the pirates?" Vanellope wheedles.

"It does seem like a lot more **fun**," you say. "And much more our cup of tea."

You and Vanellope rush to the railing and start waving.

"Yoo-hoo!" you shout. "Pirates! Volunteers over here!"

The captain strides up to you. "What on earth are you doing?"

The mate who told you to swab the poop deck joins him. "Why don't we offer them to the pirates? Since they want to go anyway. And that way the pirates will be less likely to take our other mates."

"Good idea," the captain says.

"We think so, too," says Vanellope. She high-fives you. "Pirate ship, here we come!"

Join the pirates on **PAGE 278.**

You decide to stay on point and find that steering wheel.

Your fingers fly as you type in all the info and send it out across the **information superhighway**. You're clicking and cutting and pasting and pulling down menus and swiping and tapping a mile a minute. You're moving screens so fast it's making even *you* dizzy!

"Okay, my army of netizens are all on the prowl for that steering wheel. All I have to do is sit back and wait for the hits." You stretch and clasp your hands behind your head as you lean back in your chair. "Any minute now . . ."

Wait on PAGE 104.

You scan **Game Central Station**, Ralph by your side. It's closing time at the arcade, so everyone is leaving their games. You recognize most of the characters as they drop out of their plugs.

Several of the Bad Guys from different games huddle together. They're probably heading to the weekly Bad-Anon meeting. Ralph sometimes went to those meetings. He used to be unhappy being the Bad Guy and never the hero.

You give him a sideways glance. You wonder if he still attends. Does he also get tired of his role, the way you're kinda bored by the sameness in your game? Maybe you two can find some excitement in this Internet place—after you find your replacement wheel, of course.

Turn to **PAGE 281**.

You and Ralph continue along the power strip.

"How are we going to get Surge to let us into the Wi-Fi plug?" Ralph asks.

You shrug. "We'll just ask him nicely to step aside. Oh! There he is!"

You charge forward, but Ralph grabs your collar, lifting you off the ground.

"Hey!" you yelp, your feet dangling. "What's the dealio?"

"You *do* know that we're not exactly Surge's favorite people." Ralph lowers you to the ground.

"Whyever would you say that?" you ask. "How can he not adore two **adorable scamps** like you and me?"

"Well, there was that time we switched plugs so folks ended up in the wrong games," Ralph says. He starts counting on his fingers. "Then you wanted to see if you could make him think the socket strip was haunted by glitching in and out. Oh—and that prank—"

"Okay, okay," you say. "But that's all in the past. I'm sure he doesn't hold any of that against us."

Ralph looks dubious. "I'm just saying maybe we need a strategy."

"Strategy shmategy," you scoff. "We'll just be our usual lovable selves."

Turn to **PAGE 283**.

"Sorry, Ralph," Felix says. "You're right. It's just gosh-darn easy to get distracted in there, with all the flashing lights, and the signs that change all the time, and the special offers and such."

"I know," you sigh. "I was there. Maybe Calhoun will have more luck."

Felix drops his ice-cream cone and his mouth falls open. "Calhoun's in the Internet?" He spins around. "I need to go back and find my wife!" He disappears back into the socket.

Surge Protector reappears. "Hey! Did someone just go in there?"

Uh-oh.

Turn to PAGE 161.

Ralph has to get back to his own game, but you plan to meet once the arcade closes in Game Central Station.

Before you and Ralph became friends, you never spent any time in Game Central Station. You were an **outcast**. You tried to stay cheerful and acted like everything was fine. You set up a pretty sweet place for yourself on the outskirts of *Sugar Rush*. But deep down, you were lonely.

Meeting Ralph changed everything. Together, you defeated the maniac bent on destroying you—and *Sugar Rush*. In the process, you discovered your princesshood. You also discovered a true friend.

Meet up with true-blue Ralph, and stroll through Game Central Station on PAGE 219.

The first thing you notice after you arrive is the crisp sea air. You take in a big whiff of the salty breeze. "Ahhhh! Invigorating." Vanellope inhales deeply beside you.

The next thing you notice is your stomach. It's not happy. In fact, it's downright queasy.

Then you notice a third thing that makes you forget about the first two: the giant wave about to crash down on you!

"Agghh!" you cry as you grab Vanellope and dash for cover. You fling open a trapdoor and duck below. You hear the wave pound the deck.

"Phew!" Vanellope says. "That big wave could have washed me away."

"What are you lubbers doing down here?" a voice booms behind you.

You turn to see a large man with an impressive mustache approaching you. He's dressed in a much fancier uniform than the sailor was.

"There was a big wave out there," Vanellope says.

He stares at her as if she's crazy.

You try to help out. "You know, big water." You move your hand in an up-and-down motion. "Really wet."

"You bilge rats get back to your posts or I'll have your hides!" he hollers.

Gulp. You believe him.

Go back up on deck on the NEXT PAGE.

You push open the trapdoor and climb back out onto the deck. "We're cool," you call down to Vanellope. "That was just one super wave."

Vanellope scrambles up the wooden slats after you. "This place is amazing," she says, making a slow turn.

You try to do the same—after all, this nineteenth-century schooner is quite impressive. Giant masts, huge sails, wooden deck. But your stomach has other ideas.

"I think—I think I need to sit down," you tell Vanellope. You lower yourself onto a trunk. "And quit turning," you grumble. "I'm already queasy."

The ship rolls up and down on the ocean, and your stomach rolls with it.

"You do look kinda **green**," Vanellope says.

"Don't quite have your sea legs, eh?" says a wizened old sailor. His uniform is a lot shabbier than the one the guy downstairs was wearing. His is patched and dingy, with rips and ragged cuffs. "First voyage?"

"And last," you say.

He laughs and clamps his callused hand on your shoulder. "You'll adjust quickly enough."

The trapdoor opens again and the gruff sailor emerges.

"Look alive, matey," the kindly old sailor hisses at you. Then he announces, "Captain on deck!" and salutes.

Turn to *PAGE 238*.

"Noodles!"

You turn and see a young girl with dark braids racing toward you. The puppy goes wild, pulling hard on the leash while barking with excitement.

The girl drops to her knees in front of you and throws her arms around the puppy. "You found Noodles!" The puppy's tail wags madly as he licks the girl's face, making her giggle.

When she looks up at you, you can see that she's been crying. "I'm from the game *Puppy Parents*," she explains as you hand her the leash. "We take care of puppies, and this one got away from me. I was so worried."

"Glad I could help," you tell her.

"Come on, Noodles, you naughty boy," she tells the puppy. "Thanks again," she calls over her shoulder as she walks away, the puppy jumping up trying to snag the leash.

You watch them go. For some reason, the puppy reminds you of Vanellope. They have the same high spirits.

But at least Vanellope is housebroken!

THE END.

You sniff a few times. "Somehow I fell out of my game. And now I don't know how to get back in!" You scrunch up your face as if you're about to cry.

"There, there," the woman says flatly. She doesn't sound at all like she's trying to comfort you. In fact, she sounds pretty **annoyed**.

She stashes the clipboard under her arm. "If you disappear from your game, I'll have so many forms to fill out I'll be filing paperwork from now till doomsday!" She presses a button under the display. A keyboard pops up—just like the one KnowsMore used to get you here.

"Ready?" she asks.

Before you can answer, she hits a button.

And you're inside *Sugar Rush*—the original edition!

Play the game on PAGE 69.

"Sure!" you tell Princess Vanny. "That will be so much fun!"

You and Princess Vanny sneak out of the vintage arcade games museum without getting caught. You get a lot of **double takes** on your way back to the main floor. That makes you both crack up. Then you laugh harder when you realize that even your laughter is identical.

You see Ralph waiting for you up at KnowsMore's kiosk. "I can't wait for you to meet Ralph," you tell Princess Vanny. "He's my very best friend."

"Any friend of yours . . ." Princess Vanny says with a grin.

Go to the NEXT PAGE.

"Stay out of sight until I call for you," you tell Princess Vanny. She ducks behind a parked e-mail truck.

You stroll up to Ralph and tap him on the back. He turns and smiles broadly. "I got the steering wheel," he tells you. "Did you have fun?"

"Sure did," you tell him. "I even made a new friend."

"Yeah?" he asks.

"Yup. And I think you're going to like her."

"Any friend of yours . . ." he says.

"Funny," you tell him. "That's exactly what *she* said." You turn to the e-mail truck. "Come on out!"

Princess Vanny pops out from her hiding spot. "Hi, Ralph!" she says.

He glances at her. Then stares at her. Then gapes at her. Then looks at you. Then at her. Then at you. Then at her.

"Two of you?" he says.

"Pretty incredible, huh?" you say. "Can't you just imagine all the pranks we can get up to now?"

"Actually, I'm almost afraid to think of it," Ralph says.

Ooooooh, this is going to be fun!

THE END.

"This is the most boring game ever invented," you complain. "And being a page in the most boring game ever invented is the *worst*!" You toss some beef jerky into the knight's pack and fasten the buckles. You're standing outside an old-timey tavern where the knight purchased provisions. You hope he's inside now taking a bath. He stinks!

You didn't realize that being a knight's page actually means being the knight's servant. Or that the avatar playing the role of the knight has never played this game before. He spent the first hour getting lost, falling off his horse, and making you clean off his trousers, since he always seemed to land in mud puddles. How can any of that be fun for him?

"I can't believe I'm stuck with this guy," you mutter.

"Tell me about it."

You whip your head around. "Who said that?" you ask.

"I did." The horse swings his head toward you. "And this time, can you be a bit gentler when you load this guy's packs?"

Go to the NEXT PAGE.

You gape at the horse. **"You talk?"**

"We all do," the horse tells you. "But never to the avatars. Unless they develop the power to speak to animals. But that only happens on the upper levels."

"There are other levels?" you ask.

"Sure. This is level one. And you're right, it's dull." The horse shakes his mane. "The upper levels get better. But I don't think this knight is going to advance beyond level two at the most."

"Which means we're stuck in the dull zone."

The horse whinnies sympathetically. "Precisely."

"So how do we help this guy advance?" you ask, stroking the horse's velvety nose. "If he moves up, things get better, right?"

"I doubt even with our help he'd get very far."

"He has to fulfill some quest," you say. "What is it?"

"The usual. Rescue a princess."

Your mouth drops open. "That is awesome!" you cry.

Solve the problem on PAGE 232.

You rub your hands together, feeling excited. You stride around the chocolate lake as you consider all the possibilities for making your game more challenging. You have so many ideas, you don't know what to try first!

You narrow it down to two: turbocharge your kart with a new fuel or turn *Sugar Rush* into a relay race! Make it a team sport.

As you pass the front of the *Sugar Rush* console, you peek out of the screen into the arcade. You don't have a whole lot of time to try something before players start to arrive.

You need to settle on **something**.

If you want to try a new super-duper fuel before the arcade opens, turn to PAGE 44.

If you want to try Sugar Rush *as a relay race, wait till the arcade closes and convince the drivers on* PAGE 31.

You find the knight inside the tavern studying a map. He's looking at it **upside down**, but whatever.

"Guess what!" you tell him. "I can get us—you—to the next level!"

He glances at you a moment, then goes back to his map.

"Really! You've already completed the most important part of your quest!"

"What are you talking about?" he asks.

You notice several other patrons are now listening. "You see . . . I'm a princess!"

You smile broadly and wait for him to become overwhelmed with gratitude *on **PAGE 268**.*

"Oooh!" She suddenly dashes to a screen showing shoes and handbags. **"I love, love, love it!"** she gushes. "I never would have thought of putting those purple boots with *that* pink backpack, but it works! This site is going to be a hit!"

"Um, lady, what about the steering wheel?" you ask.

She waves a hand at you. "Don't worry, I've got code working on it."

You're not so sure. She's looking at so many screens at once you don't see how it's possible for her to keep track of everything, no matter what she says.

"It was very nice to meet you," you tell Yesss, "but I think I'd better just go look for Vanellope."

"Check this out!" Yesss calls. She's laughing at a video of a pig on a surfboard.

As she hurls hearts at the video, you sneak away to the NEXT PAGE.

You're not sure where you are. You're not sure how to get anywhere. All you're sure of is that you've made a **mess** of things.

Maybe I should just go home, you think. Vanellope probably already found the wheel. You've been here awhile.

In fact, you realize, *she's probably waiting for me back at Game Central Station!*

Just one problem. How do you get back to the entrance to the Internet? And then back to Litwak's Family Fun Center?

You glance around. "Where are those search folks when you need them?" You scratch your head. You drum your fingers on the guardrail. "Now, if I recall, we came in through something called the router. Whoa!" As soon as you finish saying "router," a pod materializes around you. You're zipped back to where you and Vanellope started.

You dash back through the socket and into Game Central Station on *PAGE 144*.

"No one's going anywhere!" Surge Protector rushes around you. But before he can block the socket, he **slips** on the ice cream Felix dropped. He desperately tries to stay upright, but it's no use. As he slips, slides, and skids, you and Calhoun leap through the Wi-Fi socket and into the Internet.

"So, where should we begin?" you ask Calhoun. You know she prefers giving orders.

"Begin right here!" A netizen steps up to you and Calhoun. "Make millions without ever leaving your couch!"

"Back off, Pop-Up," Calhoun snarls.

He backs away, then turns and runs.

You realize pop-up ad holders are all around you. Some carry signs, others wear them. Some are screaming into megaphones; others play music loudly and shout their news over their blasting tunes. Several approach you and Calhoun.

"Incoming," you mutter to Calhoun. She whips her head around, glaring. You know from personal experience how scary her glare can be! You raise your hammer-like fists. All the pop-up ad holders scatter.

Now that the path is clear, head to
PAGE 163.

"Ah," the sailor says. "Yes. This is where you come to find the objects that were crucial to the proper running of a schooner."

"Like the supply closet," you say.

He deflates a bit. "I guess you could say that, yes."

You like supply closets. They're usually full of, well, supplies. "Interesting."

"Not really," Vanellope says.

The sailor puffs up again. "I'll have you know, young lady," he says defensively, "this game has been nominated several times for prestigious history—"

"Ever win?" you ask. You'd love to get a gander at whatever kind of **medals** they give out here.

"No," the sailor mumbles.

You feel bad for the guy. You know what it's like to feel like a loser. For medals to be always beyond your grasp.

You bend down so you can whisper into Vanellope's ear. "Hey, let's take a look around. Just so he feels a little better. Okay?"

Vanellope shakes her head, but she's smiling. "You are such a softie."

"Guilty as charged." You stand back up.

"We would like to peruse the premises," you tell the sailor. "Where would you suggest we begin?"

Go to the *NEXT PAGE*.

You're tickled by how excited the sailor gets. "Oh, there are so many **options**!" He stands beside the board, bursting with pride.

He points to an old black-and-white photo of a group of sailors. "That one allows you to experience life on a ship." Then he points to a picture of a large old-fashioned sailing ship. "That one lets you step aboard all the different kinds of ships on the waters at the time. Just tap a picture and you'll be whisked away to that part of the game."

"There's an awful lot of whisking going on in this Internet place," you say. You turn to Vanellope. "What do you think?"

She shrugs. "This was your idea. Go for it."

You turn back to the board and the eager sailor.

So what will it be?

Find out what life was like as a nineteenth-century sailor on **PAGE 223**.

Or check out what else was floating on the ocean back then on **PAGE 215**.

You stand and try to keep your balance as the ship continues to roll and bob on the water. You nudge Vanellope and she salutes with you. You didn't make a very good impression on the captain before. You should at least try to get on his good side now.

The captain squints at you and Vanellope. "You're new," he says.

"Yes, sir," you reply.

"Well, O'Brien, give them their assignments."

"Aye, aye, sir," O'Brien says, but the captain has already strolled away.

The old sailor scratches his stubbly chin and studies you. "Since you're new, I'll let you pick what **duties** you'll perform. Would you rather be swabbies, or are you more adept at rigging?" Vanellope starts to snicker.

"We choose our doo—"

You clamp your hand over her mouth. You don't think these sailors share Vanellope's sense of humor.

You have no idea what he's talking about, but he's waiting for you to decide. Vanellope just shrugs, so it's up to you.

What's it going to be?

Swabbies on PAGE 216*?*

Or riggers on PAGE 251*?*

"A well-outfitted Von Schweetz could overtake a Ralph-a-Rama"—Vanellope snaps her fingers—"like that."

The boy is scribbling in a notebook. "What kind of fuel do they use? Or are they powered by wind only?"

"The Ralph-a-Rama is powered by **hot air**," Vanellope says with a wicked grin.

"And the Von Schweetz runs on—"

Before you can answer, the sailor from the supply closet appears. "That's quite enough from you!" he snaps. "I'm sorry," he tells the boy, "pay no attention to these two jokesters."

"Darn it," the boy says, crossing out everything he just wrote.

You feel bad. "Sorry, kid. I'm sure this nice fella can help you." You clap your massive hand on the sailor's shoulder. He staggers under the weight.

He wriggles out of your grip. "I will be happy to guide you," he tells the boy, "once I make sure these two have left our site."

"Can we check out life at sea?" Vanellope asks.

"No. You must leave now, and there's only one way out," the sailor says. "In other words—exit through the gift shop!"

"Okay, okay, we're going," you say.

Ride in the pods to the NEXT PAGE.

You and Vanellope pop out of your pods into a noisy, bustling location. A giant neon sign overhead reads **eBAY**.

"I wonder where the bay is," Vanellope muses. "I don't see any water."

You are in some kind of warehouse filled with rows and rows of stalls containing old maps, compasses, ships' wheels, and even some old treasure! In each stall someone is shouting, "Who wants to make a bid?" Some of the stalls are surrounded by dozens of bidders, others very few.

"All this is for old-fashioned boat stuff?" you say, gazing all around.

"Who knew there was so much," Vanellope says. "Or that so many people had a thing for creaky barnacle-covered artifacts."

"I see you have an interest in ship history," the gentleman manning the booth in front of you says.

"What makes you say that?" you ask.

He points behind you. You turn and see the door you came through. It's labeled NINETEENTH-CENTURY SCHOONERS. "Oh, right."

"I have the finest artifacts hearkening back to the days—"

Vanellope cuts him off. "Do they sell other things here, too? Newer things?"

"Well, yes. But to history aficionados like you two—"

"See ya!" you say. You and Vanellope hurry away.

Turn to **PAGE 252**.

You and Ralph turn to the Wi-Fi plug. Uh-oh. Surge Protector has blocked off the plug with caution tape. Before you and Ralph can go in, you'll have to get around it.

You take a deep breath, ready to dive into that plug, when you feel Ralph's hand on your arm, holding you back.

"What's up, dude?" you ask.

"Do you really think we should go there?" Ralph asks. "What if we never, ever come back out?"

You hate to admit it, but he has a point. You're about to enter a great big unknown. You stop and think a moment. "If we don't go in," you say finally, "*Sugar Rush* could be gone forever. It's a risk I have to take."

"Okay, little sister," Ralph says. **"It's Wi-Fi or bust."**

Turn to **PAGE 200**.

You straddle the bike, but your knees come up to your ears when you sit. You hop off. "You're too small," you say, "and I'm too big."

You study the bike. You make a few adjustments, raising the seat and the handlebars. "I'll try again."

"Hurry!" Vanellope says. "It looks like all the riders are lining up at the starting line!"

She's right. You see an enormous crowd gathering and a giant banner up ahead. People line the sides of the road. *This is a very popular race*, you realize. You notice helicopters overhead and TV news crews swarming the area.

"Wow. This race is big news," you say.

"Don't get stage fright on me now," Vanellope says.

Turn to **PAGE 124**.

You rush to **Game Central Station** and find Vanellope. "Hi, Vanellope!" you say. You're so excited you can barely contain yourself. You can't wait to see your plan in action.

"Hey, Ralph," she says. "So, what's on the agenda for tonight?"

You make a big show of shrugging and sighing. "Just a regular night around here. Nothing new ever happens at old Litwak's old arcade," you say.

"I guess you should head into *Sugar Rush*."

"But we're done for the day," she says, surprised. "Aren't we going to hang out?"

"Oh, I have things to do."

"You do? Like what?"

That stumps you.

Come up with an excuse on **PAGE 14.**

244

A tall man wearing a robe and pointy hat and holding a staff watches the activity. He has such an air of **authority** you assume he's in charge. "What are they doing?" you ask him.

"They're getting ready for their adventures," he says in a deep, gravelly voice. "They arrive as themselves. Once they get here, they dress up as the characters they want to be in the game. If they collect enough talismans, they move on. Provided they survive, of course. There are many dangers here, as well as glories galore."

"Cool," you say, watching an avatar transform into a centaur. "Can I have a costume, too?"

"Perhaps, small one," he says. He peers down at you. "Who might you be? Are you visiting from another game?"

"Uh, yeah . . ." you reply. "I hope that's okay."

"Just be careful," he warns. "This is a land populated by strange and wondrous creatures. Many are friendly, but others are woefully dangerous. And the avatars—they have different strengths and skills. They will challenge you to duels and ask you for help with their quests."

"Quests?" That sounds intriguing. "What kind of quests?"

Go to the **NEXT PAGE.**

"Some will battle dragons to take their treasure," he tells you. "Others will rescue princesses."

"How about **princesses** rescuing **dragons**?" you suggest. "That would be more my style."

He ignores your comment and simply eyes you up and down. "Your attire is unusual for this realm," he says.

You have a feeling *you're* unusual for this realm.

"I suppose you could pass as a page to a knight going on a quest," he says.

"That could work," you say.

He uses his staff to point at your head. "Or, if we added points to your ears, perhaps you could take on the role of an elf."

Which will it be?

Do you want to be an elf? Get fitted for ears on PAGE 264.

Do you want to be a knight's page? Get ready for the quest on PAGE 229.

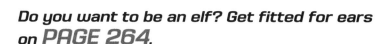

"Feisty, aren't you?" she comments. She starts to slip her smartphone into her purse.

"I'm sorry," you say quickly. "It's just—I'm kind of in trouble. And it's making me pretty stressed."

She nods knowingly. "Stress seems to be **trending** all the time!"

"I really do need help," you say. "I have to find the steering wheel for the arcade game *Sugar Rush* or it's going to be unplugged forever. Sold for parts." You try to fight it, but a tear trickles down your cheek.

A hot-pink hankie appears in Yesss's hand. She gives it to you as she nods sympathetically.

Blow your nose, then go to PAGE 287.

"Great!" she cheers. "Intel is coming in fast and furious. Don't you just love it? Information superhighway on overdrive! Just how I like it!"

Her energy is **overwhelming**. But she sure knows her way around this Internet place. She seems to be getting results. But you're exhausted!

Maybe you should just let her take over the search while you take a nap on PAGE 85.

Or maybe you should thank her and go back to looking on your own on PAGE 233.

You stand up behind the table. "Any questions before we get started?"

One skinny green **tentacle** goes up.

"Yes?" You consult your clipboard. "Yes, Cycloptopus?" You're not sure which of his many eyes you're supposed to look at. You settle on the giant one in the middle of his face.

"What do we win?" he asks.

"Win?" you repeat, surprised. "Ralph's the Bad Guy in this game. He never wins anything."

You cover your ears as the Bad Guys erupt in protest. Felix grows pale and nervous beside you.

"Oh, settle down!" you shout. "C'mon. You're Bad Guys. What'd you expect?"

You watch as most of the group files out.

One of the bad guys stops on his way out.

"Yes, Satan?" you ask a little nervously.

"That's _Sa-tine_," he corrects you. Your knees knock a bit. He's an intimidating character. His vivid red skin, large and lethal-looking horns, and towering height make him a very impressive Bad Guy.

"We thought we'd finally catch a break," Satine says sadly. "We thought by joining a new game, we'd have a fresh start." He whips his cloak around himself and stalks away.

Go to the NEXT PAGE.

You eye the remaining group. The robot with the saws
instead of hands. Zombie. And the green candy from
Sugar Rush, Sour Bill. He's been staying with you since
they unplugged his game.

"Not so promising anymore," you mutter.

Sigh. Turn to PAGE 292.

"We better stay together," you say. "Besides, it's a lot more fun to explore new places with a **friend**."

"So true!" Ralph plants his big hands on his hips. "But what new places should we explore?"

There's so much to see, your eyes don't know where to land! Monorails rumble overhead, connecting this central area to parts unknown. Elevators on gigantic buildings travel up and down. Vehicles zip past you so quickly your hair rustles in the breeze. It seems like everything around you—from avatars to blinking lights—moves at top speed.

Your kind of place!

"There's a *lot* going on here," Ralph comments.

"It's all moving at the speed of . . . well . . . *me*!" you say.

Ralph laughs. "Figures you'd like it. All the colors. The rushing around. Reminds me of a certain game I know." He winks at you.

"Which reminds *me*," you say, "I guess we better start searching."

"Search?" someone behind you asks.

Find out who said that on **PAGE 171**.

You look up at the rigging. "No problem," you tell Vanellope. "I climb the giant apartment building in my game all the time." Luckily, you've gotten your **sea legs**.

Vanellope scampers up into the ropes. "I'll race you to the crow's nest!" she shouts down at you.

"You're on, little sister!"

You grin and grip the mast. You start to climb up when a big wave makes the boat roll. You grab the ropes for balance and send one of the massive sails swooping across the deck. The sailors throw themselves down to avoid being hit.

"Ooops! Sorry about that!" you call down.

You see some of them waving fists at you. You suspect it's a good thing you can't hear what they're shouting.

"C'mon, slowpoke!" Vanellope calls.

You start climbing again.

You hear creaking. Then you hear cracking. You glance down. The sailors are still yelling up at you, but you're so far above the deck you can't hear them. Some seem to be waving at you to come down.

Then you hear the fellow in the crow's nest above you shout, "You're too big! The mast can't handle your weight!"

Uh-oh. That creaking sound you hear is the mast cracking in two.

The next thing you know, you're splashing down into the water.

Turn to PAGE 211.

"I can't see anything," Vanellope complains. "It's too crowded."

Vanellope glitches up to your shoulder and surveys the place. "If any place is going to have a steering wheel for *Sugar Rush*, it's going to be this place."

"Do you think they have a map or something?" you say. "We've been doing a lot of walking and my feet are pretty tired."

Vanellope squeals. "Sweet mother of monkey milk!" she cries. "There's a booth dead ahead. Vintage Arcade Games." She ruffles your hair. "I do believe we found what we're looking for."

"Of course we did," you tell her. "That was my plan all along. Didn't I tell you? We just had to take the scenic route, via the nineteenth-century schooner."

"Doofus," she says, grinning.

You thud through the crowds of avatars to the booth.

There, as if shining from within, is a glowing hologram of her *Sugar Rush* steering wheel.

Turn to PAGE 297.

"You deserve a break," you tell Miss Nanny. "My wife and I will be right back to **babysit** for you."

"Really? That would be great!" She smiles appreciatively, then returns to her game.

A few minutes later you return to *Baby Bonanza* with Calhoun. You take your wife's hand and ride up through the plug into the game.

Miss Nanny rushes over to you but stops when she sees Calhoun. "Um, you don't exactly look like babysitters."

"Oh, yeah?" Calhoun takes a menacing step forward. "Something wrong with the way we look?"

"No, no," the woman says hastily. "It's just that he's carrying a hammer." She points at you. Then she addresses Calhoun. "You're wearing some kind of battle gear. It's my job to keep the babies safe." You admire Miss Nanny's courage. You love your wife, but you know she can be pretty intimidating.

"We would never let anything happen to the little ones," you promise.

"Safety's my middle name," Calhoun says.

You turn to her, surprised. "Really? I thought it was Jean."

Go to the NEXT PAGE.

"Well . . . if you're sure," Miss Nanny says, still eyeing you both.

"We're sure," you say. Calhoun nods decisively.

Suddenly, Miss Nanny seems to be in a big hurry. Almost as if she's afraid you might change your mind. She bustles about, grabbing her coat and pocketbook. "The little dev—er, **_darlings_** have kept me on my toes all day." She plops a hat on her head. "They're all asleep now, but if they wake up, watch out."

She stops and studies you and Calhoun. "I hope you can handle it."

"I'm sure we can," you assure her, taking Calhoun's hand.

She rattles off instructions so quickly that you barely register that she's gone.

Then you and Calhoun are alone. With a dozen babies.

Go to *PAGE 162.*

You get the delivery info from Ralph, then tap a bunch of keys on your phone. Just as you thought, you were able to get several people to tackle every step of getting that steering wheel to the arcade. **"Done!"**

You turn to Ralph, smiling. He doesn't smile back. He just stands there, shoulders slumped, head down.

"What'samatter, big guy?" you ask. "We got you your wheel. You'll be Vanellope's hero!"

"But I don't know where she is," Ralph confesses. "And I don't know how to find her." He makes a broad gesture at all your screens. "This place is huge!"

You've always loved the possibilities that the Internet offers. The expansive, unlimited opportunities. But you suppose to someone visiting for the first time, it could be overwhelming. Intimidating.

"I have an idea," you tell Ralph. "Let's use this Internet for what it's so good at: connecting people."

"How?"

You smile. "You'll see."

Turn to *PAGE 177.*

You help Ralph and Vanellope figure out how to meet back up at **the Search Bar**. You accompany him, fearing he could get lost on the way. He does seem pretty distractible, and he definitely doesn't know the ins and outs of the Internet.

Up ahead, you see a small girl with a ponytail and a mismatched outfit. As soon as they spot each other, they charge at each other. Ralph picks the girl up in a big bear hug. When he puts her down, you join them.

"You must be Vanellope," you say.

"The one and only," she says with a grin. "Thanks for all your help. We never would have found the wheel—"

"Or each other—" Ralph cuts in.

"—without you."

"Think nothing of it," you tell them. "I love putting my expertise to good use."

Turn to PAGE 143.

"I'm Ralph," you tell her. "Who are you?"

For a moment she looks shocked. "You don't know who I am? Why, I'm **Yesss**!"

That's a weird name. "Yes? Like no?"

Her mouth twists as if she tasted something sour. "Not at all! No and I, well, we couldn't be more different."

"Ooo-kay." Does anyone in this Internet place make sense? And wasn't she wearing a different dress a minute ago? You could swear it was white when she first appeared. This one's red. And now she's wearing sleek glasses.

"I'm the head of algorithm here!" she continues. "I know it all—if it's hot and when it's not anymore. What the next big thing will be and what's going to flop. Where all the best news is, and how to find anything and everything and if it's worth finding at all. If I like it, so do you! And you and you and you!"

"Uh, who are you talking to?"

"Everyone out there!" She snaps her fingers and dozens of screens appear all around the two of you.

Turn to **PAGE 271.**

You trudge to the finish line, bracing for Vanellope to read you the riot act. Not only did you mess with her game, your shenanigans made her lose.

"Ralph!" you hear her shout.

She and the other drivers are still in their karts at the finish line. Great. She's going to scold you publicly. You've got to face the music sometime. Might as well be now.

"Listen, Vanellope—" you begin, your eyes firmly on your big feet.

"Ralph, were you behind this?" she demands. She climbs out of her kart. "All the changes?"

No point in denying it. Besides, you can't lie to your best friend. "Well . . . uh . . . kinda, yeah . . ."

She flings her arms around your legs. "Thank you, thank you, thank you!"

"Huh?" You pick her up so you can meet her eyes. "You liked it?"

"It was awesome!"

Phew!

"But you didn't win," you say as you put her back on the ground.

"Who cares?" She twirls and bounces around. She can barely contain her energy. "It's about the ride! About the challenge! Living in the moment!" She seems truly delighted. Which delights you.

"Better luck next time," Taffyta says to Vanellope. She perches atop her kart hood. Her medal dangles from her fingers as she holds it up to admire.

Go to the **NEXT PAGE**.

Vanellope grins. "Next time, luck won't have anything to do with it," she replies. "It will be pure skill."

"You mean you want us to do it this way again?" you ask.

"Not exactly *this* way again," she says. "Keep us guessing."

Calhoun, Felix, and Gene join you at the finish line. "Did your idea work?" Gene asks.

"Did Vanellope have fun?" Felix chimes in.

"Was the game more exciting for her?" Calhoun asks.

Turn to *PAGE 23*.

You open your eyes after the obstacle course, shifting gears and stomping on the gas. You give Taffyta an exaggerated yawn as you pass her.

Suddenly, you come across a sign that's never been there before. It points you to a **brand-new track**! You take it, following a homemade track over Rocky Road and the Hot Fudge Bog. You're loving it, taking the turns at incredible speeds.

But then you miss one.

You struggle with the wheel, but it's not cooperating. You career off the road and land in a ditch, stuck in a chocolate puddle.

Ralph hurries to your side. "Kid, are you okay? Jeepers! I didn't think that would happen."

You hear Taffyta calling for you. Ralph helps you out of your kart, and together you follow Taffyta to the start of the race.

All the citizens of *Sugar Rush* are crowded around the screen, peering out at Litwak's Family Fun Center. When you and Ralph arrive, they part to let you pass.

"Anyone know what happened?" you ask.

"What did you do, Ralph?" Taffyta asks.

"He was just trying to make the game more exciting," you say. "Leave him alone." You're sure that's why he did it. You were just complaining to him about *Sugar Rush* not being challenging enough anymore.

Go to the NEXT PAGE.

You watch Mr. Litwak scratch his head as the girl who'd been playing *Sugar Rush* in the arcade holds up the detached wheel.

"Oh, it's okay, Swati," Mr. Litwak tells the girl. "I think I can get it back on there pretty easy."

You hold your breath as Litwak tries to get the wheel back onto your console. Instead, it **breaks**. Your stomach twists.

Litwak studies the broken wheel. "Well, I'd order a new part, but the company that made *Sugar Rush* went out of business years ago," he says.

"I'll try to find one on the Internet," a boy says hopefully.

"Me too!" The other children crowd around.

A moment later Swati holds up her phone, beaming. "I found one!"

Your heart lifts. It's all gonna be okay!

Litwak peers at the phone. His jaw drops. "Are you kidding me? How much?" He shakes his head. "That's more than that game makes in a year."

Litwak hands the phone back to Swati. "I hate to say it, but my salvage guy is coming on Friday, and it might be time to sell *Sugar Rush* for parts."

You realize Litwak is heading toward the back of the game.

"Everybody run!" Ralph shouts. "Litwak's gonna unplug your game! Go! Run, run, run!"

Rush to the NEXT PAGE.

The drivers shriek and scream as they race out of the game. You all tumble through the plug and into Game Central Station. Several are **crying**.

"What will happen to us?" Taffyta wails.

Your heart sinks. You glitch, but it feels different this time. Could it be true? Could it really be game over for you and everyone else in *Sugar Rush*?

No way. You are princess of *Sugar Rush*—or president, or emperor, or Lady High and Mighty of All the Sweets, depending on your mood. You have a responsibility for everyone in your game.

Turn to PAGE 272.

"I think we should skip this one, kiddo," you tell Vanellope.

She crosses her arms. "You just don't want to do it because there's no **medal** for winning."

She's not all wrong but not entirely right, either. "No," you protest. "Didn't you hear what she said? The race takes *three weeks*! We can't stay out of our games for that long. No matter how much fun we're having."

She sighs. "I guess you're right." She kicks a pebble in the road. "I just hope there will be a game for me to go back to."

"We just have to find the right wheel," you tell her.

Try the wooden wheel on PAGE 208.

The wizard provides you with plastic tips to make your ears pointy. "You are a passable **elf**," he declares.

"Do I have magic powers?" you ask.

"No," he tells you. "You are but a guest in this realm. Only we who are from this place have these abilities. There are rules for you to follow. You are masquerading as a magical creature but have no powers. As such, you may confuse the avatars, since you will be unable to provide any spells they may request. Please keep to the less populated areas and all will be fine."

I don't want to be fine, you think. *I want to have fun!*

As if he can read your mind, he adds, "I believe our realm will offer you many adventures. Even with these restrictions."

You touch your pointy ears gently. "Okay. Where should I start?"

The wizard pulls a small crystal ball from his robes. "Hmm. There's a war in progress, several duels, and avatars waiting to ambush a dragon. Those are all situations to be avoided by an outsider. You should head . . . that way."

He holds out his staff and directs you into the forest.

You heard him. Get going to PAGE 212!

Mr. Hawaiian Shirt steps back. "Of course not. Why would I? I'm here to get a replacement part for my *Hero's Duty* game. A knob fell off."

"Oh," you say, dropping your fist. "That's okay then."

It takes a while, but finally you and Ralph make the necessary arrangements.

"We did it!" you say. "I can hardly believe it."

"I know," Ralph says, beaming. "I think we can safely say today we rule the Internet."

"I don't know . . ." you say. "I'll only believe it once that steering wheel is safely delivered to Litwak's and *Sugar Rush* is plugged back in."

"Then let's head for home!" Ralph says.

On the way back to Game Central Station, you worry. You may have found the steering wheel, but did you find it in time?

Find out on the NEXT PAGE.

The next day you wake up to discover you're covered by a blanket of bricks. "Wh-where am I?"

Then you remember. *Sugar Rush* was unplugged. The racers from your game are scattered. You spent the night in *Fix-It Felix, Jr.*

Ralph is snoring on the other side of the dump. You put an end to that.

"Wake up!" you yell. "We have to see if *Sugar Rush* is going to be junked or saved!"

He rubs his eyes sleepily. "Okay, okay, hold your horsepower." He frowns. "Wait a sec. The arcade is closed today."

"Oh, nooooooooooooo!" you wail. How are you going to wait until tomorrow?

You're so anxious you keep glitching.

Glitch to PAGE 135.

"What do we do?" Calhoun asks, racing up and down the rows. She looks as **frantic** as you feel.

"Take a deep breath," you tell her. You grip the railing of the crib in front of you and try to take your own advice. You breathe in and out. But you can't block out the wails of the babies. Or your wife's rather colorful muttering.

"Okeydokey, the only way to do anything is one hundred fifty percent," you say. You take in another deep breath for courage. Then you reach into the crib and pick up the red-faced baby.

The baby instantly stops crying!

Turn to PAGE 206.

You're suddenly surrounded. And the knight doesn't look particularly grateful. More like disgusted. Angry.

"How dare you **impersonate** a princess?" he demands as he rises from his seat.

"But—"

Rough arms grab you.

Moments later you're tossed into a dungeon.

"Now this princess really *does* need rescuing," you mutter.

You sigh and plop onto the ground. "I guess I should have stuck to the plan."

THE END.

The giddy avatars traveling with you to the sparkly castle are obviously thrilled. You spot a banner hanging over the broad entryway. ""**Oh My Disney,**"" you read.

As the moving sidewalk takes you across a moat, mermaids and dolphins splash in the water. A beautiful rainbow crosses the sky behind the main turrets.

The minute you walk through the castle doors, the avatars scatter, disappearing through the archways lining the massive stone hall. They all seem to know exactly where they want to go. You figure they must be regular visitors.

"Welcome!" a cheerful voice announces. "You may reach all locations from this main hall. If you have any questions, the information booth is right up ahead. We are always happy to help you. Have a magical day!"

Turn to PAGE 109.

You hear something that sounds like power coming on. A kind of **hum**.

"Hey," Ralph exclaims holding out his arms and gazing down at them. "We're green now!"

"You're right!" You hold out your arms, too, then look around. The room is cast in a green glow. "Weirdness." Suddenly, a shape zips by you and stops a few feet away.

Ralph grabs your arm. "Don't go near it! It's a gremlin!"

You watch as the blob turns into something you recognize. Rather, *someone* you recognize. "Doesn't that look like a teeny-tiny Mr. Litwak?"

"User ready!" the mini Litwak bleats.

You fall backward, startled, as he is suddenly encased in a pod and zooms away.

"Follow that little Litwak!" you cry.

Chase it to PAGE 147.

Yesss taps her glasses. "These babies keep me up to date on **everything** and **everyone**."

She frowns. She snaps her fingers and, suddenly, she's wearing a slick purple jumpsuit and a short pink jacket.

She catches you staring. She grins. "Gotta stay ahead of the trends," she says. "That red dress just appeared on the *Celebrity Who Wore It Best* show. Which means now it is just so yesterday."

She points at a screen behind you. "Oooh, we should go check out what's going on over there!"

She drags you to PAGE 79.

You turn to Ralph. "We have to take care of this."

"We do?" Ralph asks.

You give a sharp nod. "We do. It's my **duty** to—"

Ralph cracks up. "You said **doodie**."

"Shut up," you say, but you can't help giggling. You force yourself to be serious again. This is a serious situation. "I have to make sure everything is A-okay in *Sugar Rush*. I have to get a replacement wheel."

"But how?" Ralph asks.

Hmm. What did those kids say? Where did they say they found the wheel? The Internet.

"We have to go into the new plug-in," you tell Ralph. "The Wi-Fi! Surge said that's where the Internet is."

Just then, Surge Protector rushes over, hearing all the commotion. When he finds out what's happening, he tells all the *Sugar Rush* citizens they can hang out in Game Central Station until the arcade closes. After that, they'll stay in *Fix-It Felix, Jr.*

You know you'll need to *sneak* into the Wi-Fi plug. Surge made that very clear this morning.

So you and Ralph will just bide your time . . . and then into the Internet you'll go!

Turn to **PAGE 222.**

You sigh. You can't risk Litwak shutting down your game. "Let's see if we can find anyone else to try out," you say.

"Sweetums, aren't you done yet?" Calhoun, Felix's wife, calls as she arrives in your game.

You grab Felix's hand. "Why didn't we think of this before? Your wife! She'd be **perfect**!"

"Oh, I don't know," Felix says. "She's tough, sure. But she's no Bad Guy."

"Sergeant Calhoun," you say, ignoring Felix's tugs on your sleeve. "Think you'd like to give our game a go?"

"You want me to audition to be Ralph's replacement?" she asks.

"I'm sure you won't want to," Felix says nervously. "Think of all the extra work."

"My soldiers can handle some of my duties," she says. "Could be a good challenge. Besides, it might be nice to work together."

"But too much togetherness—" he begins.

You cut him off. Why is he trying to talk her out of it? "Why don't we just give it a little test run?"

"I'm game!" she says.

"Tell her what to do," you tell Felix.

Why's he so nervous? He's drenched in sweat.

Go to the NEXT PAGE.

"She's **magnificent**," you say, awestruck, as you watch Calhoun tear through the tasks. Her "I'm gonna wreck it" was so terrifying you actually shivered, and her specially designed weapon blasts bricks and windows in nothing flat.

You punch Felix lightly on the arm. "You afraid you won't be able to win anymore if Calhoun is the Bad Guy? You'll have to up your fixing game."

He tugs at his collar and gulps. "Noooo, that's not the problem."

"So what is?" you ask.

"I'm afraid we're about to find out," he says.

Turn to PAGE 290.

You and Vanellope are deposited by your pods on the side of a country road. "What the . . . ?" You look around. "This doesn't make any sense. How would looking for a wheel bring us here?"

You hear cheering in the distance. A moment later a group of bikers zips by.

"It's a **racing** game!" Vanellope exclaims. She jumps up and down with excitement. "Oooh. Let's get in it!"

"Uh, in case you didn't notice, those were bicycles, not cars."

"My first kart used pedals," she huffs. "This is going to be a cinch!"

"I hate to point out the obvious," you say. "But we don't have bicycles. Kinda crucial for a bicycle race."

"Aww, pshaw," Vanellope says. "We'll figure out something."

"But the race already started," you say, pointing in the direction the cyclists went.

A woman approaches you. "Silly big man," she says with a thick French accent, "those cyclists were just warming up."

"You mean we can still enter the race?" you ask. You kinda hope the answer is no.

Go to the NEXT PAGE.

The woman eyes you both skeptically. "You want to compete in the **Tour de France**? The most famous and *grueling* bicycle race in the world?" She snorts. "You won't last three miles, much less the three weeks!"

Vanellope's eyes grow big. "You race for three weeks straight?"

"Does the winner get a medal?" you ask. You do love your medals.

"They win money," the woman replies. "I'm not sure about a medal."

Vanellope turns to you. "Should we enter the Tour de France?"

If you want to sign up for the bicycle race, go to PAGE 294.

If you think you should check out the wooden wheel instead, go to PAGE 263.

But she doesn't. Instead she just zooms around in the spaceship. She flies straight up, then flips and does a nosedive. Her stunt flying is making you so nervous you clutch your **topsy-turvy** stomach.

She executes a series of rolls as she brings the spaceship up high again. The aliens arrive in greater numbers now. You hear her squeals of delight as she careens through the blasts.

"Shoot!" you shout. "Vanellope, quit flying around and shoot down the aliens!"

Zip to PAGE 59.

Soon you and Vanellope are aboard the **pirate ship**.

"I can't believe we have to swab the stupid deck here, too!" she complains.

"I know!" you huff as you swish your mop back and forth. "I thought we'd be counting gold coins, singing sea shanties, and going up to people and scaring them by saying 'Argh' in their faces."

Oh, well.

Life at sea isn't at all what you expected in . . .

"Woo-hoo!" You swivel back around to face forward. The kart zips along the track so quickly, everything goes by in a blur.

"Awesome!" you cry as you narrowly miss slamming into a candy cane tree. It takes all your skill to stay on the track.

Now this *is a challenge*, you think. You can't believe it! You're already nearly at the finish line. This must be a speed record!

You barrel up the final donut hill with ease. As you burst over the crest, you have so much power you're airborne!

Gulp.

You gaze down and see all the drivers staring up at you. You yank the steering wheel hard. You can't risk crashing on top of your friends! They're all shouting and pointing.

What goes up must come down. You land with a hard thud in a pile of marshmallows. The poof of powdered sugar coating the pillowy sweets makes you cough, but at least they cushioned your landing.

Turn to **PAGE 35.**

Better hold off on making any changes right now. **Litwak's Family Fun Center** is opening soon.

When it does, you join the other drivers heading to the starting line. The quarter alert resounds through the game.

"Drivers, start your engines!" the loudspeaker bleats.

Taffyta guns her kart's engine next to you. "You're, like, going down today, Vanellope."

"Did you have a big bowl of delusions for breakfast, Taffyta?" you scoff. "I could drive with one finger and still beat you."

"Three, two, one, go!" the announcer yells.

Taffyta and the others take off. You lean back in your seat with your hands clasped behind your head. "Let's give her a little head start."

As you watch the others drive away, you think back to yesterday. The new plug-in. A thing called Wi-Fi Litwak added to Game Central Station. You're curious about what it might be. Surge believes it's dangerous and has banned you from going into it.

Which makes it very, very intriguing.

But first, you have this race to win.

You do your usual ho-hum high-speed drive along the track. Yup, there's the gumdrop obstacle course. It's all so familiar you could do it with your eyes closed.

So you do.

Drive to PAGE 260.

You and Ralph stroll along the sockets acting innocent. You don't want anyone in Game Central Station to know what you're up to. Two reasons: You don't want anyone ratting you out to Surge—even by accident. And you don't want the drivers of *Sugar Rush* to get their hopes up, in case you fail.

Ralph whistles, and you hum tunelessly. "Just two friends out for a walk," you say whenever you pass anyone. You soon arrive at the **Wi-Fi socket** and stop.

"Is the coast clear?" you ask Ralph out of the side of your mouth.

He looks one way, then the other. "Hang on!" Ralph warns out of the side of *his* mouth. "Nicelanders approaching."

Go to the **NEXT PAGE***.*

You turn to see Felix and Gene from Ralph's game sauntering toward you.

"Hello there, Ralph. And Miss Vanellope," Felix says. "We just wanted to come over to express our condolences."

"For what?" you ask.

"Rumor is *Sugar Rush* is on its way out," Gene says.

"Not if we have anything to say about it," you declare.

"What can you do?" Felix asks. "We heard the steering wheel broke off and Mr. Litwak doesn't think he can find a replacement."

"Don't believe everything you hear," you scoff.

"Yeah," Ralph puts in. "Rumor is, there are steering wheels to be found in the **Internet**. So that's where me and my pal are going!"

Oh, well. There goes your plan to keep it a secret.

Turn to PAGE 298.

Ralph follows you as you stroll toward Surge Protector. He's on duty, patrolling the power strip that all the games in the arcade are plugged into.

You slow down when Surge Protector spots you. Maybe Ralph is right. That is some glare Surge is giving you, and you've experienced more than your share of glares. You gulp, but press forward.

"Why, hello there, Mr. Protector," you say as politely as you know how.

"Hello," he replies suspiciously. With good reason. You and Ralph aren't exactly known for your good manners.

You frown at Ralph. You're stumped. You don't know where to go from here.

He frowns back. Then he gets that mischievous look in his eye that you know so well. "Hey, Surge," he says, "are we glad to see you! We want to report some malfeasance over there!"

Brilliant! You put on a super-worried expression. "Yeah," you say, "we saw some undesirables causing a real **donnybrook** over there."

"A malfeasance-based donnybrook, you say? Oh, heck no. Not on my watch. Appreciate the tip!" Surge Protector says.

You watch as he hurries away.

Now it's time to get into that plug!

Turn to **PAGE 241.**

"Back off!" you shout. "Or my pal there is going to smash you all into code."

"You heard her!" Ralph stomps around waving his giant hammer hands. The aggressive search engines back off.

As they move away, you spot a little guy cowering behind a counter. He wears a bow tie, a black gown, and a square hat. The counter has a keyboard built into it. You have a strong suspicion he's another search engine.

"You!" You stalk over to him. "We've got something we've got to find and we're on a schedule."

"I could tell," the little guy says, adjusting his glasses.

"You could?" Ralph asks. "How?"

The guy shrugs. "I know things."

That sounds promising. "We need a replacement part for—"

Before you can finish speaking, the guy says, "A car?"

A picture of a car pops up on the counter in front of you.

"No?" he asks. "A kitchen appliance?" One after the other, pictures of refrigerators, microwaves, and a hot plate appear and disappear. "A knee or a hip?" He eyes you a moment, then says, "No, you look fine, fine."

"What's with this guy?" Ralph asks.

Turn to **PAGE 160**.

You stroll through Game Central Station with the adorable golden retriever puppy. You stopped by a pet shop game and the owner kindly provided a collar, a leash, and a week's supply of puppy chow. Turns out the little pup didn't come from the game, so you'll need to keep him until you can figure out where he belongs.

"Whoa, there!" you exclaim as the puppy drags you across the vast hall.

"Stop that," you scold when you pause to greet Surge Protector and the puppy keeps jumping up on him. "He's a cute little dickens, isn't he?" you say apologetically to Surge.

Surge doesn't respond; he just smooths out the wrinkles the puppy made in his trousers.

"Shhhhhhh," you say, gripping the puppy's leash tightly when he starts barking, snapping, and growling at the group of Bad Guys huddled by the information kiosk.

"Ooooopsie!" You frown down at the puppy when you realize he just peed on the floor. "Well, that's not good."

You pull a rag from your tool belt. When you kneel down to clean up the mess, the puppy dashes away, dragging his leash behind him.

You quickly clean the floor and drop the rag in the trash can. You stand with your hands on your hips, scanning Game Central Station. "Now where could that little prankster have gone?"

Find him on **PAGE 88.**

You and Vanellope enter the plug and step onto the moving sidewalk.

"Right, eBay," you say. "We go there, get the wheel, and have it delivered to Litwak before Friday. He'll fix your game. Everything goes back to the way it was. *Boom.* Happily ever after."

Vanellope gazes up at you, impressed. "This is a shockingly sound, well-thought-out idea for you, Ralph. No offense."

"I know," you say. "And none taken."

The moving sidewalk takes you to a place labeled ROUTER. You don't know what it means, but you don't want to admit that to Vanellope. Not after you just impressed her.

You step off the sidewalk and gaze around the cavernous space. *Now what?* you wonder. This doesn't look like a place to find a steering wheel. Or much else, for that matter.

"I gotta admit, I'm underwhelmed," Vanellope says.

Suddenly, the room glows green and the ground beneath your feet rumbles.

You stare as a teeny-tiny version of Mr. Litwak zips by you. He blasts down to a loading platform, where he's encased in a pod, and vanishes with a *whoosh!*

"Come on, Ralph, let's follow him," Vanellope calls, running after it. The moment her feet hit the loading dock, she's encased in a pod and zooms away.

Chase her to PAGE 192.

"I am sure I can solve your problem," Yesss says. "That's me! Always positive. Tell me more about this game."

You swallow and nod. "It's the best game in the world. We zoom through an amazing **candy** landscape. My friends and I . . ." Your throat gets tight again, thinking about the other drivers. You force yourself to continue. "*Sugar Rush* is one of the oldest games in the arcade."

"Aha! Excellent!" Yesss says. "Vintage arcade games are always a hot category."

She taps some buttons on her phone. "Just getting the word out. We should have some answers soon."

You feel like you're going to burst waiting to hear. You frown. Just a few hours earlier, you were complaining that your game was boring. Now all you want is to wrap your fingers around that wheel and drive that oh-so-familiar track. You feel bad that you have been taking your game for granted. You vow never to do it again.

She holds the phone so you can see the screen.

"That's it!" you cry. "That's my steering wheel. Where do I go to get it?"

"Just tap the screen," she instructs you. "It will take you right to eBay!"

You touch the screen. A pod wraps around you and you're whisked away.

Arrive on **PAGE 168.**

"Think about it," he says. "When a million-trillion birds are all together, what do you end up with?"

You twist your mouth, thinking. Then it comes to you. "A million-trillion pounds of **bird poop**!"

Ralph nods solemnly.

You take a few steps back. "Thanks for the warning."

"We're visitors here," Ralph says. "I doubt we'd make the best impression covered in bird poop."

"You are on a roll, buddy," you tell him. "So full of good sense, I barely recognize you."

"What?" he says. "Those birds are tweeting so loudly I can't hear you!"

You tip your head in the direction you came from. He nods.

Move away from those noisy birds on PAGE 112.

You glance up at Vanellope, who still sits on your shoulder. She's biting her lip. That's her **thinking** face.

"Whatcha got in mind?" you ask.

"Just wondering . . ." she begins, turning her gaze to the battling search engines.

"I think I'm wondering the same thing, little sister. You're wondering which of those search engines we should go with."

"Close," she tells you. "I'm thinking maybe we should split up. That way you can do a search with KnowsMore and I can do a search with someone else."

You nod slowly. "Cover more territory and uncover more possibilities."

"Roger, Dodger."

"On the other hand," you say, "if we split up, we might never find each other again. I mean, look at this place!"

You gesture widely, trying to convey the immensity of this Internet world.

"Good point, Lord Halitosis. We have to make a choice."

Hmm. Which is it going to be?

Should you and Vanellope split up to cover more territory on PAGE 75?

Or should you stick together on PAGE 156?

You look back at the building. The Nicelanders have assembled on top of the roof, ready to toss Calhoun into the mud puddle. That's how every game ends.

Only no one told Calhoun.

You can't watch. She battles the Nicelanders, kicking, biting, and screaming until they all scramble off the roof. And out of the game.

She stomps over to the table. "You!" She points a threatening finger at you. "Watch your back, mister. I don't take kindly to that kind of treachery."

"But—" you protest.

She ignores you and turns to her cowering husband. "And you!" But she doesn't finish her sentence. She just whirls around and stalks away. Felix races after her, shouting endearments and apologies.

You sigh. It's game over . . . for now.

THE END.

"Even better," you tell him, as you take him over to the screen. "I've decided I'm going to be your **best friend**!"

"You are?" He looks puzzled.

You shrug. "The way you described best-friendship makes it sound like a major thing. One with staying power . . ."

"Vanellope and I have been best friends for six years," Ralph says.

You gape at him. "Six years! That's practically forever in the Internet age." You consider him carefully. "Yes, this best friend thing really might last. Do we have a deal?" You hold your hand out for him to shake.

He doesn't take it. He just frowns. "But Vanellope is already my best friend. And that's kind of the definition of 'best.' There's only one."

He has a point. You have presided over many, many, many best lists. "Best" does mean the one and only.

Turn to PAGE 158.

"Okay, let's get this over with," you say.

Felix nudges you.

"I mean," you say, putting on a big fake smile, "ready for your wonderful **auditions**?"

The robot, Zombie, and Sour Bill eye each other nervously.

You and Felix hold up your clipboards. "We'll start with something simple," Felix says. "At the start of every game, Ralph shouts, 'I'm gonna wreck it.' Why don't you all give that a go?"

Sour Bill and Zombie do all right. With some coaching, they could probably do a pretty good job of yelling.

But the robot with the saws—turns out he doesn't speak. Just runs his motor.

"Sorry," you tell him. "You're disqualified."

The robot stomps away.

Go to the NEXT PAGE.

"Next," Felix says, referring to the list on the clipboard, "you'll do some wrecking. Brick breaking or window smashing. Your choice."

"How's the cough drop going to destroy the building?" you mutter. "Glare at it?"

"I heard that," Sour Bill snaps. "And I'm not a cough drop!" He bounces a few times, then smashes through a window.

"Not bad," you say grudgingly. You wave your clipboard at them. "Have at it."

Watch the audition on PAGE 84.

Even though there aren't any medals to win, you agree to sign up for the race. You can see how much it means to Vanellope.

"If you are **serious**," the woman says, "I rent bicycles to tourists. They aren't exactly racing cycles, but if you like, you may use those." She chuckles. "I won't even charge you. This I want to see."

"You see?" Vanellope says as you follow the woman to a shed set back from the road. "It's all working out!"

The woman flings open the door. "Take your pick," she tells you.

Just one problem.

"I'm too small for these bikes," Vanellope complains when you pull out several bikes for her to try. You lower the seat as low as it can go, but Vanellope's feet still dangle inches above the pedals.

"You can ride on my handlebars," you offer.

"Okay, let's try that."

You put her bike back into the shed and pull one out for you.

Turn to PAGE 242.

The next morning, you're a little worried. Will you really be able to pull this off?

Once you get started, you realize being the **Bad Guy** is a whole lot of fun. You get to stomp, yell, and break things. You'll also be thrown off the building, but no biggie. You can handle it. You're ready. Excited, even.

"Quarter alert!" sounds through the game. You dash into position.

"I'm gonna wreck it!" you shout. *Not bad*, you think.

You're not as strong as Ralph, so you've come up with your own strategy. You were planning to stick to breaking windows, but then inspiration hits.

You pick up one of the pies cooling on the windowsill—and smash it into Miss Green's face. "Wh-whaa . . ." she sputters as whipped cream drips down her cheeks.

You race to the next pie. "Boysenberry?" you shout. You pull it off the sill and stomp on it. "Nobody likes boysenberry!"

"My word," Mr. Carmichael says, watching you from his window.

"This is great!" you exclaim. You shout about every little thing that has ever bugged you. In fact, when you hear that Ralph and Vanellope have returned with the replacement wheel, you're a bit disappointed. You just worry a bit that maybe you went too far.

Being bad can get people mad at you in . . .

 *THE END.*

"You're telling us you're from the future?" Princess Vanny asks you.

You've just spent the past half hour describing all your adventures. And explaining that there are **other versions** of *Sugar Rush* in the world, including yours.

"I guess I am," you say. "Your game console is in some kind of museum. But as soon as someone decides to buy you, you'll be up and running again."

"Your game sounds a lot more fun than ours," Minty says, pouting.

"Only one way to find out," you say with a grin. "How about a race?"

"You mean without any human players?" Princess Vanny says. She looks concerned. "You do realize we're not in an arcade, right?"

You gape at her and look at the others, surprised. "You mean, you don't do anything during your off-hours? No racing?"

You're shocked!

Turn to **PAGE 93.**

"Isn't it **beautiful**?" Vanellope gasps.

"It sure is," you say.

You look down at Vanellope's beaming face, and you beam back. The two of you accomplished what you set out to do. Together, you found her replacement wheel.

And you also found out that no matter what, Vanellope will stay your friend, through good times, bad times, and weird times. And that everything is better when you and Vanellope are a team. You are the true-bluest of true-blue friends. And that's what really matters most in . . .

THE END.

Gene and Felix both look shocked. You don't have time for these naysayers. Surge could be coming back, and you don't know how long it will be before Mr. Litwak calls those junk dealers!

You spin around to face Ralph. "You with me?"

There's a bigger question. And it's for *you*, reader.

Are *you* going to go into the Internet?

Do you want to go on as Vanellope and head into the Internet to find a replacement wheel? Go to PAGE 220.

Or do you think someone should stay here and keep an eye on things at the arcade? Turn to PAGE 4.